PRAISE FOR

THE MINOR MIRACLE

"*The Minor Miracle* is major fun! Noah and his super crew may stretch the laws of physics with their fantastic feats, but it's the friendships that give this story its true power. You will find yourself rooting for Noah—and laughing out loud—all the way!"
—CHRISTINA SOONTORNVAT
BESTSELLING AUTHOR OF *THE TRYOUT*

"A fresh, fun, and fantastic take on what it means to be a superhero!"
—CYNTHIA LEITICH SMITH
AUTHOR OF *ANCESTOR APPROVED* AND *SISTERS OF THE NEVERSEA*

"We might think we know all about superheroes, but Meredith Davis gives us a spectacular new one—Noah Minor. In a plot filled with twists and turns, readers will discover that superheroism isn't always about saving the world using extraordinary powers. Sometimes it's about saving your best friends, and that requires the most amazing power of all: love."
—KATHI APPELT
NEWBERY HONOREE AND NATIONAL BOOK AWARD FINALIST

"*The Minor Miracle* has everything! Superheroes, bad guys, epic trumpet solos, slam dunks, and hilarious hijinks galore. It will make your heart **ZING**!"
—MAX BRALLIER
#1 *NEW YORK TIMES* BESTSELLING AUTHOR OF *THE LAST KIDS ON EARTH*

THE MINOR MIRACLE

THE AMAZING ADVENTURES OF NOAH MINOR

WRITTEN BY MEREDITH DAVIS
ILLUSTRATED BY BILLY YONG

WATERBROOK

The epigraph Scripture quotation is taken from the Holy Bible, New International Version®, NIV®. Copyright © 1973, 1978, 1984, 2011 by Biblica Inc.™ Used by permission of Zondervan. All rights reserved worldwide. (www.zondervan.com). The "NIV" and "New International Version" are trademarks registered in the United States Patent and Trademark Office by Biblica Inc.™

Text copyright © 2024 by Meredith Davis
Jacket art and interior illustrations copyright © 2024 by Billy Yong

All rights reserved.

Published in the United States by WaterBrook, an imprint of Random House, a division of Penguin Random House LLC.

WaterBrook and colophon are registered trademarks of Penguin Random House LLC.

Trade Paperback ISBN 978-0-593-44534-1

LIBRARY OF CONGRESS CATALOGING-IN-PUBLICATION DATA
Names: Davis, Meredith (Meredith Lynn), author. | Yong, Billy, illustrator.
Title: The Minor miracle: the amazing adventures of Noah Minor / by Meredith Davis; illustrations by Billy Yong.
Description: Colorado Springs: WaterBrook, 2024.
Identifiers: LCCN 2023028650 | ISBN 9780593445334 (hardcover) | ISBN 9780593445358 (ebook)
Subjects: CYAC: Ability—Fiction. | Family life—Fiction. | Adventure and adventurers—Fiction. | Great-uncles—Fiction. | LCGFT: Action and adventure fiction. | Novels.
Classification: LCC PZ7.1.D3834 Mi 2024 | DDC [Fic]—dc23
LC record available at https://lccn.loc.gov/2023028650

Printed in the United States of America

waterbrookmultnomah.com

2 4 6 8 9 7 5 3 1

First Edition

Book design by Jenny Davis

TO MY OWN PERSONAL SUPERHERO,
MY HUSBAND, CLAY DAVIS

WITH GREAT POWER THERE MUST ALSO COME—GREAT RESPONSIBILITY!
—*Amazing Fantasy* #15

GREATER LOVE HAS NO ONE THAN THIS: TO LAY DOWN ONE'S LIFE FOR ONE'S FRIENDS.
—*John 15:13*

ANDY   DAWSON   OLIVIA   SAUL

PROLOGUE

A reporter, covering the Macy's Thanksgiving Day Parade preparations, sits on a bench, taking notes.

A behemoth beagle, a supersized sponge guy, and a colossal clown loom over the crowds in Central Park who've come to watch the annual inflating of parade balloons.

As he gazes up, he notices a man standing on a balcony, illuminated by the full moon. The man locks eyes with the reporter, then extends his arms over the rail.

The reporter's pencil hangs frozen over his notepad. *Could it be? No.*

Yes, the man is holding a baby!

"Hey!" the reporter yells. His shout is easily drowned out by the chatter of the crowd, the churn of generators pushing air into balloons, and the honking of cars.

It takes a second for the reporter to register what he sees next. He breaks into a sprint, knowing he'll be too late, but he runs anyway, panicked. His eyes stay on the baby falling belly up, with legs and arms churning. It's as if everything is in slow motion, but the reporter still can't move fast enough.

He knocks down a metal barricade—which clangs to the ground—dashes across the street, and scoops up the crying infant from the sidewalk. There's not a scratch on the baby's tender, pale skin, but he continues to cry, his arms reaching to the night sky, where the full moon hangs, reflected in his light blue eyes. Everyone is talking at once when a woman runs out of the building, screaming.

"Move over! Let me through!" The woman takes the baby from the reporter and holds him tight. "Oh, Noah, Noah," she croons.

The man from the balcony breaks through the crowd, his eyes filled with tears too. They're light blue, just like the baby's.

"You dropped him! I saw you!" accuses the reporter.

"I'd never!" the man insists. "I'm his great-uncle. I love him like my own son! I turned my eyes for one second, checked my phone, and when I looked up, Noah was crawling through the rails."

A stylish older woman joins the throng. "It's all my fault! It's an old building . . . not up to code. I should have—"

"That's not important now," says the great-uncle. "What we need to be asking is, How did he survive?"

As the reporter watches and listens, he begins to doubt what he saw . . . because, really, who would drop a baby off a balcony? By the time his headline runs, the only thing the reporter is sure of is that something mysterious and amazing happened in the park that night.

A "Minor" Miracle in Central Park?

Nine-Month-Old Noah Minor
Mysteriously Survives Sixteen-Story Fall

I have always loved comic books, but if my life were a comic, it would have only one panel: me falling sixteen stories and surviving.

When I was little, I thought I might be a superhero. I was all about capes and trying to fly. **ZAP! BOOM! THWACK! THE MINOR MIRACLE SAVES THE DAY!** But I'm twelve years old now, too old to keep pretending. Superheroes are for comic books, not real life.

Most of the seventh graders at Rim Rock Middle School don't even know about my miraculous survival. To them, I'm nothing special. I'm just an average kid standing outside the library with my two extraordinary friends, Haley and Rodney, waiting in line to have our vision tested. Does it bother me? Yes. But I've got a plan that should earn me a spot among the gifted and talented at our school.

"Check out the dance flyers." Haley points to a flyer with glittery letters hanging on the wall.

Come to the
Starry Starry Night
Christmas Dance
December 17

"I came up with the theme at our student council meeting." She gives her ponytail a tug, keeping her straight light hair neat and tidy and under control, like everything in her life. She makes straight As, spikes volleyballs for our best team, and serves as our seventh-grade student council representative. Basically, Haley is perfect.

"Hey, maybe I can put a band together to play at the dance," says Rodney. He plays trumpet in our school band, *and* he's cool. Pretty extraordinary for Rim Rock, where those two things don't usually go together. Especially since most days he also has a circle imprint on his lips from doing his cheek-stretching exercises. His goal is to have cheeks that inflate as big and round as his jazz trumpet idol, Dizzy Gillespie, so he keeps a mouthpiece in his pocket for practicing.

"Thanks, Rodney, but we're getting a DJ." Haley flips open her planner. That's right—she brought her planner to the annual vision testing. It's like a security blanket for her, except less soft. She loves to fill all the boxes on the calendar with things to do and then draw little lines through them when they're completed. Volleyball practices, karate twice a week at her dad's studio, student council meetings, homework, chores. She records it all.

"December 17 gives people ten weeks to ask a date. If they want to." She counts the boxes on the calendar.

Rodney makes googly eyes at us.

"Stop it, Rodney," we say in unison, and then I fist-bump with Haley. He loves to tease us about being a couple someday, but Haley is more like a sister than anything. We've known each other since we were in diapers.

"The three of us are going together like last year, right?" I ask.

"I'm down," says Rodney, but Haley is too busy looking at her planner to respond.

"Noah, you've got your first basketball practice tomorrow." Yes, she even puts *my* activities in her planner.

"I know. I got this," I tell her, and myself. Rodney and Haley know about my big goal to be seen as more than ordinary. I'll make headlines again. Maybe not *The New York Times*, but I'd settle for the *Rim Rock Record*, our school newspaper. This week I found out that I made the A team as a seventh grader, so I'm on my way. It's usually only eighth graders on our school's best team, but Andy Kho did it last year, and it made him pretty famous. At least at Rim Rock Middle School.

"Hey, Noah," says Rodney, pushing his dark-framed glasses up his nose. They have no prescription, but he thinks they make him look more like Dizzy. "Maybe I could play at your games!" Out comes his mouthpiece, and Rodney blows a buzzy sound with his own signature swagger, his cheeks inflating like he's squeezing two Ping-Pong balls. Up and down the line, kids grin at him. It's like a middle school superpower, the way Rodney can make people happy.

Suddenly, the door to the boys' bathroom down the hall bangs open and The Tormentor, aka Chuck Gallusky, steps out. He's an eighth-grade bully who walks around the school like he's a god, just because he plays football and basketball and runs track. He's one of the few kids at school who shaves, and he wears tight shirts so everyone will notice his big muscles. Oh yeah, and he's my new teammate.

I look for the teacher who's supposed to be watching us in the hall, but she's nowhere to be found.

Rodney is still *buzz, buzz, buzz*ing on his mouthpiece.

"Rodney, cut it out!" I mutter. Chuck loves to torment all sorts of kids, but band kids are an especially favorite target.

Rodney plays louder. *Buzz, buzz, buzzbuzz, BUZZ!*

I yank on his arm, which pulls his mouthpiece away from his lips. "It's Chuck."

"The Tormentor?"

I cringe at Rodney's loud voice. I told him never to use our name for Chuck in public! I cringe harder when Rodney turns and they almost collide.

"Nice lip ring," Chuck says.

"Thanks." Rodney touches the indented circle. "These lips are solid gold."

Chuck glances around, then grabs Rodney's mouthpiece and holds it above his head.

What an insufferable clod, I think. Some of my best insults are inspired by my comic books, but I don't say them out loud as much anymore.

"Dude!" Rodney tries to leap up and grab his mouthpiece, but he's too short.

I'm not. I've grown six inches already this year. I reach to grab it, but before I can get a hand on it, Chuck backs into me, knocking me off-balance. Hot anger rises in me, fast and explosive, and I feel like a shook-up soda ready to explode. I take a step to keep from falling, and Chuck never even turns around.

Villain! Scoundrel! Scourge of the earth!

More heat floods my body, cheeks to toes, and suddenly I feel squeezed.

Trapped.

My clothes are tight and uncomfortable, sticking to me like I have static electricity.

It's The Cling. It sometimes happens when I get walloped with a surge of emotion. It's unpredictable, and nobody really understands it. The doctors never even came up with a name for it, but they deduced a strong emotion, like anger or fear, triggers it. I could have told them that.

Chuck is focused on Rodney and doesn't notice. "You must be in dorkestra!" he taunts.

Haley taps Chuck on the shoulder. "He's in band, not orchestra," she says.

"Yeah." I try to sound as confident and cool as Haley while I pull at my clinging clothes. Mistake.

Chuck ignores Haley and zeroes in on me, his eyes locking on the way my clothes cling tightly to my body. "What are you? Some kind of freak?" he asks.

OOF!

A few kids giggle.

"He's so weird."

"What's wrong with him?"

I hear their whispers. Everyone is now staring at my stupid clothes... and my red-hot face.

"No, I'm your teammate." I wish I had a cleverer comeback.

Chuck sneers. "Oh yeah? I don't remember seeing you."

That's impossible. We tried out together, and we're on the same team. He must have seen my name on the roster. "I'm Noah." My voice cracks. I clear my throat and try again. "Noah Minor."

Chuck is at least three inches shorter than I am, but I feel like he's growing more powerful by the second as he harnesses all the dark forces of middle school. "Well, Minor sounds like the perfect name for a nobody," he says with a villainous grin.

"Ha!" Someone behind me laughs.

"You've never heard the name Minor?" Rodney jumps in. "Noah's dad was Ted Minor. There's still a bunch of trophies by the gym with his name on them, and there are even some downtown at the university."

It's nice that Rodney has my back, but I kind of hate that he threw my dad's name out there.

Chuck raises his eyebrows, looks me up and down, and says, "Well, he didn't pass on his genes, because if you were that good, I'd know who you were. Why don't you buy some clothes that fit and stay out of this?" He gives me a shove. It doesn't matter that he needs to reach up to do it. He is still filled with a stupid amount of confidence, and he makes me feel like a little kid.

I'm still trying to think of a clever retort when a familiar voice says, "Comin' through," and Andy Kho parts the small crowd like God parting the Red Sea. "Hey, Noah."

At least *he* remembers my name.

Andy grabs Chuck's arm. "Dude, you can't be fighting in the hall. Coach will kill you if you get a detention and miss practice."

Chuck gives Rodney and me a final glare but allows himself to be led down the hall and around the corner. I swing between relief and humiliation.

"Back in line!" says the teacher, who finally appears when she's no longer needed.

"I really think student council needs to do an anti-bullying campaign," says Haley.

"What a jerk," mutters Rodney. "He still has my mouthpiece."

"What a feckless dolt."

"Good one!" Rodney loves my comic book insults.

He lowers his voice and asks, "What's with The Cling? Why is it still"—he pulls at my shirt, releases it, and watches it stick to my skin again—"clinging? It's lasting a lot longer than usual."

When I was little, The Cling ran through me fast, like a shiver or gasp, and was gone in seconds. Rodney came up with our name for it. He says it sounds like a cool villain name, as in **THE CLING ATTACKS AGAIN!** But there's nothing cool about my clothes sucking to me like they just came out of the dryer. And lately it's been happening more frequently and lasting longer too.

"It's getting worse."

"I wonder if it's because of"—Rodney glances at Haley, then whispers a little too loud—"puberty?"

I push him away from me, and Rodney laughs. Haley studies her dance poster like she has no interest in discussing puberty in the hall either.

Rodney comes close and lowers his voice. "Don't let The Tormentor bother you, man. Just calm down. Relax."

I take a deep breath, and The Cling slowly fades. My clothes gradually peel off my skin as the heat drains out of my face.

"Hey, band dude!" calls Andy from down the hall.

Everyone, including the teacher, turns to look at him.

"Yeah?" says Rodney.

"Catch!" Andy tosses Rodney's mouthpiece like he's shooting a three-pointer. A shot so perfect that all Rodney has to do is open his hands and catch it.

"Andy is such a good guy." Haley hugs her planner to her chest as he disappears around the corner again. If this were a comic book, the speech bubble coming out of her mouth would say, **MY HERO!**

The letters on the bottom line of the eye chart taped to the library wall are so tiny that I have to really squint and concentrate to see them.

"F, E, Z, Q—"

"That's enough," the doctor interrupts. He's staring at a device that looks like a fat phone with dials instead of buttons, and his white lab coat doesn't fit right. It stretches tight across his broad chest and big biceps. "Follow me, Noah."

"Is something wrong?" Nobody has ever had to talk to me about my eye test before.

"We'll go in here." He opens the door of a study room that is just large enough for a round table and six chairs. I start to get a little nervous. Why couldn't he say whatever he needed to say in the library?

"Sit," he says, pulling out two of the hard wooden chairs and turning them to face each other. I sit in one, and he takes the other. "My name is Director Wolfshaw." He holds out his giant hand for a handshake. He squeezes my fingers hard as he shakes twice and then releases. "Let's get right to it." He leans forward, elbows on his knees and hands clasped. "I work for Gravitas: a covert international organization that partners with the CIA."

"CIA, as in *the* CIA?" I'm so confused. Why would the CIA be doing eye tests? Wolfshaw watches me, as if my reaction is being tested. "And what is Gravi— What did you say?"

"Gravitas. It's an elite organization that protects and defends all that is true, good, and beautiful in this world. In the last month, we exposed a ruthless dictator's lies by slowing his escape from authorities, saved hundreds of innocent lives by diverting the path of a bomb, and saved a large portion of a national park by pulling rain clouds over a wildfire."

I swallow hard. *Is this for real?*

"We identify and recruit students from all over the country by imbedding microscopic sensors in the eye charts the government distributes for the seventh-grade vision test. While you were reading the letters on the eye chart, the chart was reading you. Your test indicates that you, Noah Minor, are a gravitar."

My heart beats hard and fast, and I can feel my pulse in my fingertips, hear it pounding in my ears. I struggle to keep my voice steady. "A gravitar? What does that mean?"

"It means you have the ability to manipulate gravity."

Please, God, let this be real, I pray as I stare at Wolfshaw, waiting to see if he starts laughing.

But he doesn't laugh. Instead, Wolfshaw points to a can of pens and pencils in the middle of the table. "Watch this." The can falls over with a clang. Then one of the pens slides across the table and into Wolfshaw's open hand.

**AMAZING!
FANTASTIC!
INCREDIBLE!**

He's not flying or shooting a web out of his wrist, but still!

"You mean I can do that? I have . . . superpowers?"

Wolfshaw shakes his head. "No."

OOF!

"You absolutely do not have superpowers," Wolfshaw says firmly. "A gravitar's abilities are possible because of science—not the bite of a radioactive spider, some magic ring, or any other superhero hocus-pocus."

"But then... how did that can tip over and that pen move without you touching them?"

"I used my pull—a simple manipulation of gravitons. It's the first skill a gravitar learns."

Okay, so not superpowers. But I *do* have abilities, or whatever he wants to call them. I can't believe it! I'm an elite. Chosen. Special. It's hard to remain calm. I want to run down the halls screaming, "I told you! I knew it!" Nobody will forget my name once they see what I can do.

Wait... what *can* I do?

"Can gravitars fly?"

"No." Wolfshaw's expression is serious. "We push off the ground, which may *look* like flying to the untrained eye." He leans back in his chair and crosses his arms across his chest. "We've had our eyes on you for a while, Noah."

"You *have*?"

"Ever since you made headlines for surviving that sixteen-story fall."

"Are you telling me that I used my powers to save myself?" Finally, the mystery is solved!

But Wolfshaw frowns and shakes his head. "No. There's no way a gravitar who hasn't been aligned and trained could use their abilities. Let alone a baby gravitar."

"Then how—"

Wolfshaw holds up a hand, cutting off the rest of my question.

"Your great-uncle Saul dropped you, and then he saved you."

"He dropped me? Uncle Saul said I *crawled* off the balcony. He said he couldn't get to me fast enough." That's what I've been told my whole life.

"Saul is a liar."

Wolfshaw stares at me as I try to digest my new history. Why would Uncle Saul drop me, only to save me? And if he saved me, that must mean... "Uncle Saul is a gravitar too?"

"That's right. He worked for Gravitas as a scientist, and he had a theory that gravitar legacies—those with gravitar relatives—could be more powerful if they were identified and trained as infants. But when he said the babies would need to be exposed to a life-threatening event to induce an adrenaline rush, Gravitas refused. We presume he dropped you to test his theory, but then he disappeared."

Wolfshaw keeps talking, his words falling like *Tetris* blocks, so quickly that I barely have time to make sense of them. "Saul's idea was not only unethical; it was also incorrect. Gravitas scientists are convinced that, legacy or not, adrenaline doesn't enhance a gravitar's powers. And he isn't just unethical and reckless. He's a thief. The night he disappeared, Saul stole some sensitive information. But he needs the help of aligned and trained gravitars to access it. As a family member, you're his best bet. Have you seen him? Has he contacted you?"

I quickly shake my head. "No! No, sir. He disappeared the night I fell . . . I mean, the night I was dropped. My parents told me he had some sort of top-secret job with the government and had to go underground once his identity was made public in that *New York Times* article. None of us have seen him since."

Wolfshaw squints his eyes like he doesn't believe me. "We suspect he'll be reaching out to you soon and will want your help. When he sends you this year's snow globe, we'll need to check it for bugs."

"You know about those?" One arrives in the mail each year around the anniversary of my fall, always from Uncle Saul, with no return address.

"Of course. We've already swept your house for bugs, and so far it's clean."

I flush, thinking about the tub of superhero stuff I keep under my bed. Do they think I'm immature?

"Saul will suspect we're contacting you, now that you're in seventh grade. If you think he's been in your home, or if you see anything unusual, let us know. We'll do another sweep. And of course, if he makes contact, tell us immediately. It's important for Saul to at least *think* you're getting aligned and trained so he'll come out of hiding."

"Wait . . . what do you mean *think*? I *am* getting trained, aren't I?"

Wolfshaw leans forward, putting a strain on his tight lab coat. "Only .0006 percent of the population possesses the ability to manipulate gravity, and an even smaller percentage is admitted to the program. We don't train every candidate just because the eye charts indicate they have the ability. Gravitas accepts those who are at the top of their class academically, athletically, and socially."

I squirm in my chair.

"They're straight-A students."

SLAM!

"Their bodies are in peak condition."

UGH!

"And they're leaders among their peers."

OOF!

"Frankly"—Wolfshaw looks me up and down—"you're lacking in our excellence indicators, and I seriously doubt you have what it takes to make it in this program."

It's not a great time for The Cling, but it never is, and I don't have any control over it. My clothes stick to me tighter than Wolfshaw's coat does to his biceps, and my whole body radiates heat.

Wolfshaw studies my pants and shirt sucked tight to my body. "Gravitas briefed me about this issue you have. Interesting." He reaches out and tugs on my shirt. It immediately clings back to my skin when he releases it.

"Maybe it's a sign of my powers!" I suggest.

Wolfshaw shakes his head. "I've never heard of this happening to any other gravitar. It's likely a mutation of your abilities—a result of being dropped at such a young age." He clears his throat and looks away, as if he can't stand the sight of my clinging clothes. "Gravitas has decided to give you a pass on your excellence indicators for now. You made the A team for basketball; that's a start. But we expect to see your best effort in all arenas, and you'll need to prove you can keep your mouth shut."

Wolfshaw pulls a rubber bracelet out of his pocket and hands it to me. It says "Rim Rock Mustangs" on it, just like the ones half our student body wears. Haley gave me one at the start of the semester, but I lost it.

"It's a bug. Wear it at school and at home, even in the shower."

"Got it." I slip it on my wrist as my clothes gently release from my body.

"It transmits what you say, as well as electronic and written communications. If you write, text, or tell anyone what you've learned in this room, you'll be suppressed."

The word sounds ominous. "What does that mean?"

"Suppression is a procedure we use to erase specific memories. If you're suppressed, you'll forget everything related to Gravitas."

He says it like wiping away someone's memories is no big deal. Part of me thinks this is impressive. The rest of me thinks it's horrifying. "Does Gravitas do that a lot? Suppress people?"

"It's mainly used when non-gravitars see something they shouldn't. Your uncle Saul helped develop the technology. *He* would have been suppressed if we had caught him before he disappeared, and so would everyone who saw that Minor Miracle. That's what the paper called it, right?"

I sit up a little straighter. "That's right."

"What a joke." Wolfshaw shakes his head.

I deflate a little.

"By the time that article came out, Saul was long gone and it was too late for suppression."

This all sounds like something out of one of my comic books. Uncle Saul is a villain, I'm about to join a top-secret agency because I have powers, and I could get suppressed if I make a wrong move.

I'm seriously stoked and can't wait for my training.

"I won't say a word about Gravitas to anybody," I promise. "And I'll tell you if Uncle Saul shows up."

"Good. Your gravitar classes will be on Monday and Wednesday afternoons. You need to convince your parents to enroll you in the beginner teen martial arts class at Black Belt Karate Studio so you can start training next week."

That's Haley's dad's studio!

"Gravitar classes are held *there*? My friend's dad owns that place!"

"Yes. It's a cover. There are regular classes in the front. Gravitas uses a room in the back."

It will be hard to keep this a secret from Haley. She can always tell when I'm hiding something. And I'm not sure how to convince my parents to let me sign up. I tried karate when I was little but dropped out after a couple of weeks. I'll have to figure it out.

"I'll be there" is all I say to Wolfshaw.

He nods, then stands, and it's clear this clandestine meeting is over. "Remember, tell nobody." Wolfshaw points to my bugged bracelet. "Behave like nothing has changed."

"Yes, sir." One thing I've always been good at is being normal. Who knew that's what it would take to prove I can be super?

3

After school, I pedal my bike hard, filled with energy. No, power. *Super*power. I coast to my driveway, dead leaves crunching under my tires, then hop off and fly through the back door.

"Hey, Mom. I'm home!" I call. She's usually home from work by the time I get back from school.

"Hi, Noah."

The Cling overtakes me. A man who is *not* my mom is sitting at our kitchen table, holding what looks like a gun; it has a wide mouth, kind of like Rodney's trumpet.

Should I run and escape? Or wrestle the gun-thing away from this guy? Fight and flight battle within me, but The Cling ultimately has me frozen, trapped, tightly held by my clothes and my fear. Sweat soaks into my tight shirt.

"Fascinating. How long has this... this thing been

happening? What do you call this condition?" he asks, pointing to my clothes.

I find my voice but ignore his questions. "Who are you? Where's my mom?" I eye the door, trying to figure out if I can get to it before he shoots. Then I remember I've got my bracelet. I just need to keep talking, and Gravitas will come save me.

"Your mother had a flat tire in the grocery store parking lot. I needed to speak to you alone."

"Please don't hurt me." My voice sounds scared.

"I would never!" He sets down the trumpet-gun and holds up his empty hands. "This is just a device that loops the sounds of your house before you arrived so Gravitas won't hear us."

This does not make me feel better.

"They're who you should be worried about," he says, shaking his head. "Don't you recognize me, dear Noah?"

The man's wiry white hair sticks out in all directions. He has a thick mustache, and the rest of his face is covered in stubble. He looks at me intently, and I notice his eyes are a piercing light blue, kind of like... mine. Those eyes stare back at me every morning from the newspaper article on my wall, but in that picture, he's younger and clean-shaven, with his hair in a military buzz cut. "Uncle Saul?"

He puts his hand over his heart. "You remember! I hoped you would."

"What are you doing here?" I ask.

"I knew this was your testing day, and I've missed you so much, Noah. But we don't have time to talk about that now. We only have a few minutes before they get suspicious of too much quiet. I can't stay long. I presume Gravitas told you some pretty horrible things about me?"

I take a careful breath. Maybe I can gather some intel and impress Gravitas. "They said that you stole some valuable information and that I didn't crawl off the balcony—you dropped me."

Uncle Saul nods slowly. "Those things are both true."

I had assumed—maybe even hoped—he'd deny it. "I could have died!"

"Ha!" His explosive, sarcastic laugh makes me jump. "You don't think I would have let you die, do you?

You're a legacy, *my* legacy, and because of that fall, you have unbelievable powers. Much greater than the average gravitar's."

Unbelievable powers? Does that mean his experiment worked? Nobody at school thinks I'm incredible, and Wolfshaw was clear that Gravitas isn't impressed by me.

My clothes begin to release, settling away from my skin.

"Please tell me about this fascinating phenomenon," Uncle Saul says, reaching out and touching my clothes.

"I call it The Cling." I still can't believe he's here, in my kitchen. There are way more important things to discuss than my freaky condition. "If I have incredible powers, why haven't I been able to use them? When I was a kid, I jumped off couches and tables and even the roof one time, trying to float or fly or do whatever I did that night. It never went very well."

Uncle Saul smiles. "What do you think The Cling *is*?"

"It's not a superpower! It's humiliating. It makes me feel like a freak."

"Ah." He nods. "But the things that make you different, even make you suffer, can be your greatest strengths. Most gravitars don't get access to their powers until they're aligned. But you? You're so full of power that it already leaks out of you, Noah. *That's what The Cling is. That fall was my gift to you.*"

Is he crazy? Nothing about my clothes trying to suffocate me feels like a gift. "Gravitas said it made me strange, not powerful."

Uncle Saul shakes his head in disgust. "They're idiots, thinking their excellence indicators tell them all they need to know about a person." He paces back and forth across the kitchen floor, running his hand through his already-crazy hair. "Don't believe everything they say."

I don't know what, or who, to believe. "I was told gravitars aren't superheroes. We can't fly or—"

"Noah, they can call it what they want, but believe me, you can fly. You can *soar.* But first, you need to get aligned. Only Gravitas can do that. And then you need to get your pull. An event is coming that will make you more powerful than even the most experienced gravitar, and I need you to be prepared."

I was already pumped to begin training, but Uncle Saul's words fill me with a new sense of pride and purpose. My very best dreams are the ones in which I can fly. I imagine myself soaring above our neighborhood, wowing everyone at Gravitas and surpassing their stupid indicators. "What event? When?"

"Patience, grasshopper. The time isn't right."

Grasshopper?

The sound of the garage door rising startles both of us. Mom is home.

"Any communication from me will be marked with this symbol." He pulls a necklace out from under his shirt and shows me the charm, round and pocked with craters. A full moon.

Uncle Saul picks up his silencer gun and shrugs on his backpack. "I left a little something for you in your room. You and me, Noah—we can change the world!" He slips out of the kitchen just as the back door opens.

Mom barges in with her hands full of bags, making so much noise that it hides the sound of the front door opening and closing. "Sorry you beat me home, honey! I stopped by the grocery store after work, and when I came out, I had a flat tire! Can you help me unload the car?"

"Sure." I glance at my bracelet. *Act normal, Noah. They're listening.*

My mind swims with questions as I carry bags from the car to the kitchen. *What if Uncle Saul isn't the bad guy Gravitas says he is? What if he's just misunderstood?* His words linger in the kitchen. *"We can change the world!"* I want to believe it.

But I'm not going to change anything if I don't get into karate. When I told Haley at lunch today that I wanted to take classes, she was super excited. We decided I should wait and ask on Sunday night, when the Fosters come over for dinner. I'll have to be patient all weekend... like a grasshopper.

After helping Mom put away groceries, I hurry to my room to see what Uncle Saul left for me. It doesn't take long to find the new snow globe sitting on the shelf where I keep all the others.

He bought my first one on the afternoon before I fell—or rather, before he dropped me—off the balcony. I don't remember it, of course, but my parents told me. I study my collection. Each one has a scene from New York: the Statue of Liberty, the Empire State Building, a yellow taxi. The new one has a big full moon, Uncle Saul's symbol, hanging above the New York City skyline.

I pick up the globe and shake it, feeling as stirred up as the white flakes that swirl inside the plastic dome. I've always looked forward to getting them each year, but holding this one fills me with dread. What if, when I take it in to be tested for bugs, Gravitas questions why the snow globe came early? I promised I would let them know if Uncle Saul contacted me. It's not too late. I could alert them to his visit right now. All I have to do is say the words, explain that Uncle Saul disabled my bug. If they hurry, maybe they could still catch him.

But what if Uncle Saul is right and I'm more powerful than any other gravitar? I won't get to find out what he knows if I turn him in.

I set my snow globe next to the others and make a decision. I'll hand it off in gravitar training on Monday, assuming I can convince my parents to let me take karate. I'll say it just showed up. If it's bugged, I'll know I can't trust Uncle Saul. If not, I'll wait until he tells me about this event that will make me more powerful than the most experienced gravitar. What could it hurt?

I'm a ball of nerves on Sunday evening, worried about whether I'll be able to convince my parents to let me take karate. When the doorbell rings, I hurry to get it. Haley's little brother, Brady, runs inside and heads straight for my room. "Noah, let's play!"

Haley and I follow him, and she asks in a quiet voice, "You ready for Operation Persuade Parents?"

"Ready."

Brady drags my top secret tub out from under my bed so we can play before dinner. He's like the little brother I wish I had, and we've loved playing superheroes together. But now Gravitas is listening, and I want to sound mature, serious about being trained.

"Can I be the good guy this time?" Brady asks, popping off the tub's top. "I know he's your favorite, but it's my turn."

I cringe. "I don't care. No biggie."

"Thanks!" Brady digs past the cape, utility belt, and spring-loaded bracelet that shoots out fake spiderwebs, then takes a superhero for himself and a supervillain for me.

"Pow! Bam!" Brady yells. When he notices I'm not playing, he pauses. "Hey, Noah, come on!"

"Yeah... maybe later, buddy." I set my supervillain back in the tub. "I'm kind of old for pretending."

"What?" Brady looks like he's going to cry.

"Noah!" says Haley, her mouth hanging open in shock.

I think fast. "You know what? You can have all this stuff, Brady."

Brady's eyes get wide. "Really?" he asks.

I glance at a comic I was reading earlier, sitting by my bed. I still love it. "Everything in the tub," I clarify, blinking back stupid tears. The truth is, I'm not really ready to part with any of it. At least I saved something.

"Thanks, Noah!" Brady gives me a big hug and then

drags my tub—I mean, *his* tub—down the hall to show his parents.

"Why did you do that?" asks Haley. "I thought you loved all that stuff!"

"Well, I guess you don't know everything." I turn my back to her, pretending to read the *New York Times* article hanging on my wall even though I have it memorized.

"Well, that was really nice of you," Haley says, being gracious despite my sass. She really is practically perfect. "Hey." I turn around to see her holding the new snow globe Uncle Saul gave me. "When did you get this?"

I must remain calm. Haley has a way of sniffing out a lie. "Yeah, it just came this week."

"He sent it early this year."

No shock that she knows this. I wouldn't be surprised if she keeps track of my snow globe arrival dates in her planner.

I keep my voice level, like it's no big deal. "Yep."

She shakes it and watches the flakes swirl. Thankfully, Mom calls from the kitchen that dinner is ready.

Haley puts the globe down and pats my back. "Time to put our plan into action!" she says, and we head to the table.

Dinner seems to go quickly, and I struggle to find

my opening. Haley keeps looking at me with raised eyebrows, but I shake my head slightly. I'll know when the time is right.

When Brady starts a competition to see who can hang a spoon off the end of their nose the longest, I decide it's finally time. Everyone is full and happy, laughing around the table as Mr. Foster wins and is crowned king of the Spoon-nosers, complete with a napkin crown. This is my chance.

I clear my throat. "Mr. Foster, is it true that karate helps you have faster reflexes?"

"It is."

"Watch this." Mrs. Foster tosses a napkin ring at Mr. Foster, and he karate chops it.

"Nice!" I pause, like I'm thinking about it. "Faster reflexes sure would help my basketball game."

"They absolutely would!" says Mr. Foster.

Dad butters another roll and takes a big bite. He isn't really listening yet, but Mom is. "Ah, honey, I don't think you have time for karate classes now that you're on the A team. You need to use your free time to keep your grades up."

I'm ready for that argument. "I read online that karate students do better in school."

"That's true," says Mr. Foster. "Studies show that the discipline required of martial arts students has a positive impact on their academics."

"Hmm." Mom glances at Dad, who is looking from me to Mr. Foster.

"You want to take karate... now?" Dad asks, finally paying attention.

"Yes! Can I take some classes at Mr. Foster's karate studio? It will help my game *and* my grades. And if it doesn't, I'll quit. I promise."

My parents stare at me like I've lost my mind. Hopefully they won't bring up the time I took classes when I was younger and quit after two weeks. Especially while I'm still wearing my bracelet bug.

"That would be so awesome," says Haley. "I've always thought Noah would be great at karate."

"And honestly," says Mrs. Foster, "I think Haley does so well in school *because* of all her activities, including karate. She's so busy that it forces her to be organized to make sure she can get everything done. Maybe you should let Noah try."

"We have a beginner teen class that would be perfect for him," says Mr. Foster, beaming.

He has no idea what's really going on in that class.

My parents look at each other and have one of their invisible conversations. Then Dad slowly nods. "As long as it doesn't interfere with basketball."

After dessert, Mom signs me up online for Monday and Wednesday afternoon classes. *I did it! You hear that, Gravitas? I did it!*

I text Rodney after the Fosters leave to tell him I'm going to do karate.

RODNEY
> You just want to spend more time with Haley

NOAH
> No way

RODNEY
> Admit it, you're crushin'

NOAH
> She's like my sister

RODNEY
> Whatever bro

NOAH
> Whatever

I don't let Rodney get to me. He'll let it drop eventually. I'm so excited, I have a hard time falling asleep that night. I read my comic and think about Uncle Saul's visit and imagine my first day in class and try not to think about the superhero tub that is now residing under Brady's bed.

Finally, I fall asleep.

I wake up with my sheets pressed tightly around every inch of me. I can't remember the details of my dream—or nightmare. Something about Chuck trying to set my comic on fire and Uncle Saul hiding under my bed. I hate when The Cling happens in my sleep. I can't kick the sheets off; I just have to wait until it goes away.

I reach out to touch the soft, thin pages of my comic and lay it across me like a colorful paper blanket. Then I imagine the story soaking down through my chest, reminding myself that tomorrow I'm finally going to learn how to be the superhero I've always hoped I was.

★★★

The karate studio is close enough that I could ride my bike, but Mom insists on driving me so she can take my picture. For every year of my life, there's a photo album lined up on a shelf in the living room, and this is the kind of thing she loves to fill them with. First days, first times—she documents them all.

"Come on, Noah. Just one."

I stand up straight in front of the sign and smile, hoping nobody from my class sees me. I guess I should be grateful that she doesn't try to come in with me.

The studio is flanked by a sandwich shop and an office building. It doesn't look very impressive, but I guess that's the point. Nobody would ever suspect that anything other than karate is going on inside. I step into a large room, and I'm instantly hit with the smell of sweaty bodies mixed with the faint scents of melted cheese and fresh bread from the deli next door.

Parents sit on wooden bleachers along the windows, watching a group of little kids on the padded black mat. They're all standing at attention, dressed in white pants and shirts and colorful belts. A few kids that look my age come through the door and cross the studio to a back hallway. I wonder if they're in my class.

"Are you Noah Minor?" asks a man in a black uniform with a black belt.

"Yes, sir." It feels right to call him sir, like I did with Wolfshaw.

"Mr. Foster said you'd be coming in. He's already in class, but he left you a uniform." The man hands me a folded black uniform with a white belt coiled on top. "You can change in the bathroom." He points to it. "And then just go down the hall, past the office. Your class will be on the right."

"Thank you, sir."

My uniform pants are way too short—hopefully no one will notice. I'm nervous enough without looking like a total dork. All the kids in the front studio were barefoot, so I figure I should be too. I shove my shoes in my backpack with my clothes and hurry across the back of the studio. I'm trying to be stealthy, but one of the kids in the back row turns and says, "Your pants are little!"

A few other kids giggle.

"Back row, attention!" their instructor barks. All the kids stand up straight with their arms at their sides, staring forward as their instructor walks across the black mat toward me. "Let me help you tie your belt."

I *did* tie it, but it looks nothing like the other belts in the room.

The whole studio watches as he ties my stiff white belt correctly so each end hangs down. It's humiliating to have a stranger tie my belt in front of all these little kids.

"Thank you, sir," I say when he's done, then hurry across the cool black mat to the back hallway. The door clicks shut behind me, and I pass the office and a few doors on my left, where I can hear kids chanting, "Cross, jab, cross, jab, jab." Haley and Mr. Foster must be in one of those classes. I keep walking all the way to the last door on the right. There's a sign that says Beginner Teen.

Should I knock?

No. They're expecting me. I belong here. I take a deep breath, count to three, and open the door.

But I must have screwed up and opened the wrong door. Standing in front of a small group of students is Mr. Foster. Did I get the wrong room?

"Shut the door, please, Noah. And you can lock it now that everyone's here."

ZAP!
WHAMMM!
KAPOW!

Mr. Foster is a gravitar? The Cling surges through my body, hot and heavy and violent as a lightning storm.

My mind races as I turn and close the door, trying to make sense of what's happened. The moment I lock it, green beams of light shoot at me from lasers that have popped up from the floor all around me. I freeze in place, afraid to move.

"Don't worry," says Mr. Foster. "The scanner is just making sure you aren't bugged."

My eyes dart to my bracelet, and I grip the straps of my backpack tighter, thinking about the snow

globe inside. What happens if I'm bugged? Poison darts? Sonic scream? Mind control? Nothing would surprise me at this point. The green lights move down my body. When they hit my feet, there's a beep and they descend into the floor.

"You're clean," says Mr. Foster.

I let out a breath I didn't realize I was holding. "*You're* a gravitar?" I ask.

"That's correct."

So at dinner, when I was convincing my parents to let me take karate, he *knew*.

Mr. Foster walks across the mat and stands in front of me. The class remains at attention, four to a row, but every eye is focused on my skintight clothes and flaming red cheeks. "Congratulations, Noah."

"Thank you... sir." It will take a while to get used to calling Mr. Foster—the man who hangs a spoon off his nose at our dinner table—sir. But something tells me that it's the right way to address him in this space.

"I'll take that." He points to my rubber bracelet. "I know we can trust you, Noah."

I pull it off and hand it to Mr. Foster, grateful that I'm no longer being monitored. Then I slide off my backpack and leave it near the back wall. I'll wait until after class to

give him the snow globe, even though I'm pretty sure it's clean after the whole green laser bug scan.

"We start class with warm-ups. Bow before stepping on the mat, and then stand on a white dot."

There are mirrors on the front and back walls, and a padded black mat covers most of the floor. Twelve white dots are spaced evenly in three lines on the mat, but the first two rows are full. Mr. Foster bows and then walks to the front of the class. I bow and take a spot in the back row by myself, which is fine. I need to watch—not be watched—until I figure out what I'm doing.

"Class, what is the purpose of Gravitas?"

"To protect and defend all that is true, good, and beautiful!" the class responds in unison. This must be the opening routine. I repeat the words in my head so that I can join in next time.

"Very good. To do this, we must have a sound mind, a strong body, and a pure spirit. We'll start with one hundred jumping jacks. Begin."

I clap and slap with the rest of the class. As my muscles get warm, The Cling recedes and my uniform settles away from my skin. Finally.

I take note of the room. By the mirrored wall behind us, there are big balls on the floor with numbers on their sides, ranging from 10 to 150. In one front corner, a thick rope hangs from the ceiling next to what looks like a red dinner bell. In the opposite corner, there's a door. A necklace with a big medallion hangs from the doorknob.

"Push-ups!"

Everyone drops to their bellies. The only sounds in the room are the blowing of breaths and Mr. Foster counting.

I take sneak peeks at the class in the mirror as I push up and down until my arms burn. There are three girls and five boys. The belts are evenly divided: four orange and four yellow. I'm the only tighty-whitey belt, with karate pants that are way too short.

"Run in place, knees high!"

I scramble back to standing and follow the command.

Mr. Foster walks to the back row and stands in front of me. "Higher." He holds his hand at waist level so I'll know where my knees should hit. I pump harder, concentrating on my churning legs and hitting his hand each time. My heart is pounding. This feels like basketball warm-ups, not gravitar training. How long till we get to the good stuff?

"Warm-ups strengthen your body and focus your attention," says Mr. Foster, as if he can read my mind. "You learn to focus your thoughts as you discipline your body."

I push myself to keep up with the class.

"Sit-ups!"

I flop to the mat on my back, wrench my head up, and let it fall back down.

"Ninety-eight, ninety-nine, one hundred. Everyone flip over! Superman!"

Superman? This sounds more like the good stuff. I sit up and watch what everyone does. The class rolls to their bellies, stretching their hands out in front of them and holding their toes up off the ground. They look like they're flying, but on the ground.

"Banana!" yells Mr. Foster. Everyone rolls to their backs and assumes the shape of a banana, holding their heads and feet up in the air, their arms still stretched over their heads.

Great—just another warm-up sequence.

"Noah, care to join us?"

I flop back and forth with the rest of the class, Superman to banana, like a fish that's just been yanked from the water. Finally, Mr. Foster tells us to stand at attention. I pull my shoulders forward so my top can absorb some of the sweat that's rolling down my back. A pretty girl with long black hair, dark eyes, and light brown skin catches my eye in the mirror and smiles. Before I can smile back, Mr. Foster starts talking again and she looks away.

"Class, shout out your names so Noah can learn them. We'll start with the first row."

There's a kid named Dawson wearing a yellow belt. He's the biggest kid in the class, but I'm still the tallest. The pretty girl with dark hair is named Olivia, and she's an orange belt. There's a redheaded yellow belt named Annie and another yellow belt named Luis. In the middle row is one more yellow belt—Amal—and three orange belts, Jayden, Oliver, and Leena.

"I'm going to explain a few things to Noah. Everyone else, grab some weights and go through our strength training drills."

Nobody moves from their spots. They just turn and face the back wall—and me. I turn when I hear something move behind me, then step aside just in time to avoid getting hit by one of the big balls I noticed earlier. Eight of them in various sizes roll forward, all without being touched! It's the first time this training feels like anything more than a regular karate class.

"Noah, I'll start at the beginning."

I drag my attention back to Mr. Foster.

"*Your* beginning," he continues. "When a gravitar is identified, they must be relocated near one of our three training facilities. A parent receives a job offer they can't turn down or some other incentive. We relocated your family after you made headlines so that you could begin classes immediately once you were deemed a worthy candidate. That's why you're our only white belt today. More should join you in January as the candidates get vetted and accepted and their families are resettled."

So basically, my family was moved like a pawn on a chessboard? I try not to let it get to me. This is how all secret government agencies work, right? And I'll have a head start on all the other white belts.

"When will I learn how to do stuff like that?" I ask, pointing to the weighted balls. Most roll slowly, but Dawson's is almost at his feet.

"The skill you are seeing is called a pull. It's the first and most basic skill, and it takes the average gravitar about two months to master."

Two months! I don't intend to be average. Not after what Uncle Saul said about my incredible powers. I bet I can do it in half the time or less. It doesn't look too hard, and he's counting on me to be ready for whatever event is coming up.

"The next two beginner skills will take a little longer. There are three skills associated with each level of training. It generally takes a year to move from beginner to intermediate, and another year to graduate to advanced."

"I'll have to wait *three years* to be an agent?"

Mr. Foster shakes his head. "More than that. You'll spend another three years running through the levels again, learning advanced variations of the skills you've already mastered."

"That's six years!" I don't know what I was picturing, but it wasn't karate class for six years. It sounds like an eternity.

"Assuming you don't fail, that is. By the time you graduate from our program, you'll also be graduating from high school," Mr. Foster continues. "Then you'll enter the military and be assigned to a top secret branch of the CIA. This is where you'll receive your final phase of training, learning practical agenting skills in the field."

"Wait... gravitars can fail?" I ask. "Like, flunk out?"

"It's very rare," says Mr. Foster with a reassuring smile. "We give students twice the average time to master each skill. But eventually, if it isn't working, we remove them from the training program."

What does that mean? Suppression? Tiny beads of sweat break out on my forehead.

"It's nothing for you to worry about right now, Noah. You just started, and I know you'll work hard."

I'll work *really* hard, but I'm still worried. What if it isn't enough?

Mr. Foster takes a remote out of his pocket and presses a button. One of the mirrors transitions into a screen. "It's probably easier to understand with this chart."

MIDDLE SCHOOL GRAVITAS BELT PROGRESSION

LEVEL	BELT TEST	SKILL
BEGINNER	YELLOW	PULL
	ORANGE	HEAVY PULL
	GREEN	SLG
INTERMEDIATE	BLUE	PRESS
	PURPLE	HEAVY PRESS
	BROWN	INTERMEDIATE SLG
ADVANCED	RED	PUSH
	GRAY	HEAVY PUSH
	BLACK	ADVANCED SLG

I try to absorb the information, noticing that white belts aren't even listed. I guess it's because all I had to do to earn it was get approved for training.

"What's an SLG?" I ask.

"We pronounce it *slug*," Mr. Foster says. "It's an acronym for 'slow-let-go.' Students must be able to gently come down from the ceiling by slowly letting go of their pull, without using the rope or harness, to earn their green belt and advance to the intermediate class. Slugging requires slowly letting go of your power, like pulling off a Band-Aid slowly or easing into a cold pool instead of jumping. It can be very difficult for gravitars who are just learning, with their powers still raw and new. Watch and I'll demonstrate."

Mr. Foster looks up and begins to rise slowly and smoothly. "This is a pull."

INCREDIBLE! It's like he's on an invisible elevator. Once he reaches the ceiling, he uses his hands to move toward the bell. He looks like an astronaut in zero gravity, propelling himself through the body of a spaceship.

"There are two ways to move sideways once you're up. In the beginning, you will continue to pull on the ceiling and use your hands to move, like I'm doing. A more advanced gravitar can pull on two objects at once, such as the ceiling and a wall, to move sideways." He rings the bell and then slowly descends. "I'm slugging now, slowly letting go of my pull."

When his feet touch softly to the mat, the class claps twice in unison. I didn't realize that they had stopped to watch. I clap a little longer, like a fan begging for an encore, because come on— that was **AMAZING!**

"Two claps are enough, Noah," says Mr. Foster. "As a gravitar, you need to keep your emotions under control."

I bristle a little but don't let it get to me. There's too much to learn to waste time on being offended. "What do you pull on if you're outside? The moon?"

"The *moon?*" Annie squeals, like I just suggested something ridiculous.

"Annie, if you have a question, you can raise your hand. I like your out-of-the-box thinking, Noah, but the moon is much too far away to pull on. To elevate outside, you would push off the ground, which is an advanced skill. I'll show you." Mr. Foster stares at the weighted balls the class was pulling earlier, and they roll to the back wall. "I used my push to, well, *push* the balls to the wall."

I glance back at the chart. I won't learn how to push for two more years! I hope I don't have to wait that long before I can fly, or elevate, or whatever they call it. Uncle Saul made it sound like it would be sooner.

"That's enough demonstration for today. Class, you may play Benderball while I get Noah aligned."

Benderball? I watch the class disperse as I follow Mr. Foster to the door I noticed earlier, wondering what cool thing they'll do next. I catch Olivia watching us in the mirror, and a look of sympathy flits across her face. This alignment thing that Wolfshaw and Uncle Saul both felt was so important is finally about to happen, and it occurs to me that it may be unpleasant.

"Is getting aligned painful?" I ask.

"It's over pretty quickly." Mr. Foster puts a hand on my back, but he doesn't answer my question.

6

Mr. Foster removes the necklace that's hanging from the doorknob. The medallion is carved to resemble the earth. He places it around my neck, and I realize it's deceptively heavy for its size.

"What's this made of?" I ask, touching it.

"A very rare, heavy-mineral meteorite." Mr. Foster adjusts it so that it rests at the center of my chest. "It's important for your force to originate from your center. The pendant will focus your abilities during alignment."

"So I just have to wear it for a while, and I'll be all aligned?" I ask. It seems a bit dorky, but less scary than I expected.

"Not quite." Mr. Foster opens the door that the medallion was hanging on. I peer inside and see… a storage closet. There's a broom, a bucket and mop, and a wall of shelves with a bunch of boxes stacked on them.

Suddenly, the boxes begin to move. Some slide forward, and others slide to the back of the shelves, all without being touched.

I look up at Mr. Foster, who is staring at the boxes intently. "Alignment orients the gravitational poles of every cell in your body in the same direction so that you will be able to direct your abilities accurately." He never takes his eyes off the boxes. "And I can't be sure, since you're the only gravitar to have The Cling, but I have a hunch that orienting your gravitational poles should take care of that little problem too."

"Really? That would be amazing." After talking to Uncle Saul, I figured it was just something I'd have to deal with my whole life—a price I'd pay for greatness. Losing The Cling will be like a bonus prize.

The boxes stop shifting. I hear a click, and the entire closet begins to rise like an elevator. An empty chamber with smooth, curved silver walls takes its place.

"Whoa! That's awesome!"

"Welcome to the alignment room."

Out of the corner of my eye, I see the students with orange belts dangling above the training room. They're wearing harnesses like the ones rock climbers wear and are clipped onto ropes that have dropped out of the ceiling. The yellow belts remain on the mat. Balls the size of softballs, but covered in holes like pickleballs, are rolling and floating around the room.

"Noah," says Mr. Foster, dragging my attention back to the silver alignment chamber. "To be a gravitar, you have to learn to focus."

"I'm ready!" I say, stepping into the chamber. Two yellow footprints show where I'm probably supposed to stand. It reminds me of the machines at the airport that do a full body scan. *Those* don't hurt.

"Good! When I close the door, raise your arms above your head."

I take a deep breath as Mr. Foster closes the door behind me. It's dark. I reach out and touch the walls. They're frigid.

"Don't touch anything, and hold still." Mr. Foster's voice comes through a speaker overhead.

I quickly take my hands off the walls and raise my arms above my head. There's a buzz, and a shock runs through my entire body, taking my breath away. A strangled wheeze escapes my throat. One time, Rodney dared me to put on a dog's shock collar; when I got shocked, my whole body went stiff, and I felt like my insides were fried. This feels like that. I breathe shallowly, my mind going numb as my body is racked by some unseen force. Gradually, the force shifts, concentrating on the front half of my body and leaving my backside all tingly.

I don't know how long I've been in here. When the shock finally stops, I fall over, exhausted.

Mr. Foster opens the door, and I stagger to my feet, putting my hands on the metal walls to steady myself.

"How do you feel?" he asks.

"A little shaky." The hair on my arms is sticking straight up. The pain is gone, but it's taken a lot out of me.

"It won't take long to adjust. Come on out, and let's make sure you're okay."

I step out of the chamber with a stumble and almost fall. As Mr. Foster takes my arm and helps steady me, I catch a glimpse of the alignment chamber descending and becoming a regular storage closet again.

"Class, let's run through a few simple karate exercises in case your parents ask to see what you've been learning, and then we'll be done."

"Done?" I ask, feeling dazed. "But I didn't learn anything." Except that getting aligned does hurt. A lot.

I get over my dizziness enough to learn how to do front and roundhouse kicks before we're dismissed. I fight back disappointment, telling myself that the next class will be better.

After everyone leaves, I pull my snow globe out of my backpack and hand it to Mr. Foster.

"Our scanners didn't go off when you got to class, so I don't think it's bugged. But it's odd that it came early this year. I'd like to take it home for further testing."

"Sure." I avoid his eyes as I hand it over.

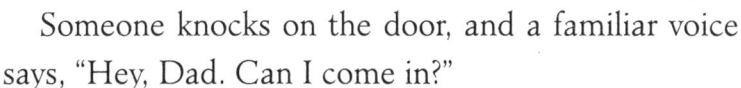

He tucks the globe into his duffel bag. "Saul was one of our top scientists, so he'd know how to hide a bug pretty well."

Someone knocks on the door, and a familiar voice says, "Hey, Dad. Can I come in?"

"Don't worry," I whisper to Mr. Foster. "I'll play it cool."

Mr. Foster nods at me and smiles, then calls, "Come on in, Haley!"

The door flies open, and Haley steps into the studio, then shuts the door behind her. Suddenly, I feel a strong force drawing me across the room. I lean backward against it, but I can't help stumbling across the mat toward Haley. What's going on? Haley has this huge smile on her face.

"Haley!" says Mr. Foster. "Release Noah!"

The pull is suddenly gone, and I fall on my butt, like I just lost at tug-of-war.

"Oops, sorry," Haley says.

I look from her to Mr. Foster. "*Haley* did that?"

"She did." He rolls his eyes.

"Surprise!" she yells.

"Wait...you're a gravitar too?" I ask, trying to comprehend what's happening.

"Yes!" She gives me a giant hug, trapping my arms by my sides, then lets go and crosses her arms across her chest, beaming. "Isn't it great?"

First Mr. Foster, then Haley. My world has been rocked so hard that I feel dizzy again. "So, who else is a gravitar that I don't know about? Brady? Mrs. Foster?"

"No, no. Just Dad and me. Check it out!" Haley rises up to the bell on the ceiling, rings it, then gently comes back down.

WHOA!

"I graduated to the intermediate class over the summer."

"But *how*? I thought Gravitas didn't train kids until they were seventh graders."

"Gravitas let me in early." She says it like it's no big deal.

I can't believe Haley has been living my superhero dream on top of the rest of her overachieving life. I shouldn't be surprised that Haley Foster got into Gravitas early, but I'm so *over* feeling inferior to her. My frustration must show on my face, because her wide grin dims a little.

"I've waited so long to tell you! Isn't it awesome?"

"Yeah, awesome." I try to match her smile. I'm still a gravitar! Who cares if Haley beat me to it?

"Hey, you don't have The Cling!" says Haley. "This kind of surprise would have caused it for sure, right?"

I look down at my clothes, which are hanging loose like any normal seventh-grade karate student's. "Hey, yeah!" Normally my clothes would be sticking to my body right now, and I'd feel like the inside of a toaster oven.

"The alignment must have gotten rid of it like you thought, Dad!" Haley says.

"I think it did. Come on, you two. We need to get Noah home. Remember, no talking about Gravitas until we're in the car, in case a regular instructor or student is still here."

Once I slide into Mr. Foster's back seat and all the doors are closed, I start asking the questions that have been bubbling inside me.

"You knew about gravitars when I took the eye test, didn't you?" I ask Haley.

"I knew you were being tested, but I didn't know if you'd be admitted into the program until Dad got the word from Gravitas," she says from the front seat.

"And of course, Haley couldn't say anything until after your first class, just in case it didn't work out."

I'm still trying to grasp the whole picture. "Did you get to start Gravitas training early because your dad is an instructor?"

Mr. Foster puts a hand on Haley's shoulder. "We needed Haley to start early because she had a top secret mission."

"Dad!" Haley says, her jaw clenching.

"What top secret mission? Can you even tell me?"

Haley slides the rubber band out of her hair and combs it back into a new ponytail with her fingers, the way she does when she's nervous. When she doesn't answer, her dad does instead.

"We needed her to watch you."

WHAM!

Haley turns to look at me and rolls her eyes. "That sounds bad. I mean, I *was* watching you, I guess, but I was already your friend, so it wasn't anything really."

Mr. Foster continues, "It was easy to convince your dad to relocate his family here since this was where he grew up. And because I had a daughter your age, Gravitas moved us down the street, so that you and Haley would be friends. We needed to know if Saul ever made contact beyond his yearly snow globe delivery. It's been a wonderful assignment."

SLAP!

The word *assignment* hits me hard. There's no way to paint this so that it looks okay. "I've been Haley's *assignment*?"

"Noah." Haley tightens her already-perfect ponytail. "That's not what he means."

"I guess now I know why you're always writing my activities down in your planner." It makes so much sense—Ms. Perfect being so interested in plain old Noah Minor.

"I've only known about Gravitas for the past year," Haley insists. Her eyes are pleading. "You were my friend way before then."

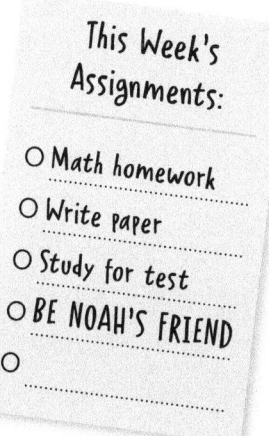

Yeah, right. Thankfully, we've reached my house. "It's no big deal."
I push open the door and slam it behind me.

Haley rolls down the window. "Noah, please don't be upset. Let's talk later."

What a *foul, faking phony* she is. Sometimes there's no appropriate comic insult, so I think of my own.

Mr. Foster leans forward. "You understand, right, Noah?"

I don't have to answer because Mom opens the front door and steps outside. "Thanks for bringing Noah home," she calls, waving.

"Sure thing. He did great today!"

"Noah," Mom whispers, "you should thank them for the ride home."

"Thanks," I say, holding up a hand.

Thanks for being good babysitters for the past twelve years.

I manage to avoid Haley the next morning, but it's hard to hide at lunch.

"We need to talk," she says.

"I'm kind of busy right now, and after school I have basketball practice. Why don't you check your planner and find out when I'm free?" I reply.

"Not funny, Noah." Haley looks like she wants to use her pull to flip me out of my chair, but all she says is "I'll text you later."

"Dude!" says Rodney, his eyes wide as she walks back to her table. "What's going on?"

"I can't talk about it." I wish I could tell Rodney everything, like I usually do.

"Well, whatever it is, promise you'll tell me if you kiss when you make up."

I roll my eyes. At least I know Rodney will never change.

After dinner, my phone buzzes with a text from Haley.

HALEY

> meet me in the park, 5 minutes

She's so bossy, but I can't avoid this conversation forever. Might as well get it over with.

It's almost dark when I get to the playground. The lights are on, buzzing softly. Haley is sitting on a swing, waiting for me. We're the only ones here.

"Hey." She keeps her voice low.

I don't respond. She looks at me with her light green eyes and holds out my snow globe. "Dad said it's fine."

"Good." My frustration bubbles up, and I finally let it all out. "I can't believe you kept this huge secret from me all this time," I say as I take the globe.

She kicks the pebbles as she swings slowly back and forth. "I hated it, but what could I do? I couldn't tell you. You didn't tell me when you found out you were a gravitar, did you?"

She has a point.

"My parents trusted me. Gravitas trusted me." Haley scoops up a few pieces of gravel and tosses them at me. "Come on—swing with me."

I set down the snow globe and sit on the swing next to her.

"I thought you'd be a little more excited."

"Excited that my best friend has been spying on me for a year and she's only my friend now because she has to be?"

"I told you; it wasn't like that. I *am* your friend. I always have been. When you were little, all you ever talked about was being a superhero. I couldn't wait for you to find out about Gravitas! Now I don't have to keep this big secret to myself anymore, and I won't have to lead this double life alone."

I twist so I'm facing her. "But when you started training, I became your *assignment*." The word catches in my throat. I turn, twisting the swing's chains tighter and ratcheting up higher. "Admit it. You had to hang out with me, even when you didn't want to anymore. And you've been spying on me, reporting everything to Gravitas."

"I haven't been spying on you." Haley digs her heels into the gravel. "I've been helping protect you."

"I don't need your protection!"

"Sh!" Haley glances around, then whispers, "Don't be so loud. And you do need protection if your uncle comes back for you."

Her controlled voice just fuels my anger. Classic Haley—always in control of her voice, her grades, her hair, and every other part of her perfect little life.

I pick up my feet, and my swing spins violently as

the chains unwind. It jerks back the other way, whipping me around before settling.

Uncle Saul was in my kitchen, and I handled myself just fine, thank you very much. I don't need Haley's protection.

"Gravitas thinks Saul could be coming for you now that you passed your eye test. It wouldn't be very hard for him to find out where you go to school and when you'd be tested. They need to catch him, Noah. He's dangerous. He's willing to terrorize babies."

Terrorize? Maybe it was scary when Uncle Saul dropped me off that balcony, but I was unharmed, and I don't even remember it.

I keep my thoughts to myself, of course. "Yeah, I know. Wolfshaw told me" is all I say. Haley doesn't know everything, and neither does Gravitas. If what Uncle Saul did makes me super powerful, like he says, I'd say it's worth it. What's a moment of fear for a lifetime of incredible power?

"Gravitas thinks *you* could be the one who draws him out of hiding."

"So they're using me as bait?"

Haley's jaw drops, and she looks at me like I'm crazy. "No!"

"Wolfshaw was pretty clear that I wasn't up to Gravitas standards. Maybe the only reason they accepted me into the program is so they can catch my uncle."

"That's ridiculous! Gravitas trusts you enough that they gave you a mission."

She doesn't know that I've already betrayed that trust, but I refuse to feel guilty for keeping Uncle Saul's visit a secret.

"They're *partnering* with you to catch Saul, not using you."

I can't convince Haley of anything, even if I tell her everything Uncle Saul told me. But maybe she can fill in some of the blanks I have about a few things. "Wolfshaw told me my uncle stole some valuable information. Do you know what it was?"

"Wolfshaw didn't say?"

"No."

Haley is quiet for a beat, then says, "You should ask Dad about it. I'm not sure if I'm allowed to tell you."

I roll my eyes. Ms. Perfect strikes again. Haley always follows the rules.

Before I can push further, she hops off the swing and runs to the giant robot that towers three stories above the playground. Two metal tube slides extend from its chest like arms, and there's a ladder inside that leads up to the head. The robot was our favorite place to play when we were little. We used to race up the slides to see who could reach the top first.

I want to go back to being that little kid who didn't

wonder whether Haley was really my friend. Who just knew it without asking.

"Come on, Noah. Let's play like we used to." Her voice echoes inside the slide.

"I don't think I can fit up there anymore."

"Just try."

I take a running start and jump into the other robot arm headfirst. I have to lie flat on my belly and grip the sides with my shoes, inching up like a worm. When I get to the top, Haley is laughing.

"Nice moves, Noah."

"What can I say? I'm good." I can't stand up all the way in the robot's chest, so I kind of crouch. We both look out through the metal bars and into the sky. It's a dark blue, bordering black. Stars are beginning to appear—faint pinpricks like Haley's freckles, sprinkled across the sky.

"I wish we could tell Rodney what's really going on so he—"

Haley cuts me off. "You can't tell anyone! You understand that, right? Not Rodney, not your parents."

"I know, I know. Top secret, confidential." I didn't say that I *would* tell Rodney, just that I wish I could.

"But we have each other, and

we can talk about the stuff we can't say to anybody else. Having this secret makes us closer friends than ever."

I look at her green eyes, shining in the moonlight, and I see the Haley I've always known and trusted. I feel a pang of guilt for being so angry with her. "Yeah, that's pretty nice."

I sit down on the metal platform inside the robot belly. Does keeping Uncle Saul a secret from her push us further apart? Haley not telling me about being her assignment felt like a betrayal, but this secret feels different.

"How long did it take you to get your pull?" I ask, changing the subject.

"Three weeks."

"That's fast. Your dad says it takes the average gravitar two months to get their pull."

"Yeah. I think it happened faster because I'm a legacy. Maybe it will with you, too, since you're also a legacy."

"I hope so. Your dad didn't even show me how to pull yet. Yesterday was just an intro."

"Be patient and trust the process, Noah. You're going to be an awesome gravitar."

Haley has always believed in me. She's never made fun of my superhero obsession and always picks me first for her team when we play kickball with the neighbors. She was sure I'd make the A team, even when I doubted myself. I could add *being a good friend* to the never-ending list of her perfections. The thing is, sometimes it's hard to be around people like her.

She hops into the left robot arm and slides down. I spin around and slide down the right one, trying to beat her, but she wins. As usual.

"So, are we okay?" asks Haley.

"Yeah, we're good."

But we'll be even better if I can get my pull in less than three weeks and—for once in my life—beat Haley.

8

On Wednesday afternoon, the class starts another game of Benderball while Mr. Foster shows me a training video on the screen in the mirror. I don't know what I expected, but it wasn't an old woman in a knitted sweater, sitting at a wooden spinning wheel with a ball of wool in her lap.

"Understanding how a ball of wool becomes a single thread was helpful to me when I was learning how to pull," Mr. Foster says. "Notice how it twists and condenses into one long thread."

The old woman pumps at the pedals of the spinning wheel and slowly feeds the ball of wool into it.

Is he serious?

"Every gravitar finds their own way to their pull. For me, I remembered when my grandmother let me help her spin wool. The tug of the thread was deeply ingrained in my fingers, and it helped me spin gravitons the same way."

Please don't tell me I'm going to spend my second day of training watching a grandma spin wool. I glance at the rest of the class in the mirror. I'm not able to track all that's happening, but it looks way cooler than what I'm doing.

"How do you play Benderball?" I ask, eager to get to the good stuff. "What are the rules?"

"Remember, Noah, you need to focus if you're going to get your pull. We'll get to Benderball later. First, I want you to watch this video a few more times and think about what's happening."

I stifle a sigh. How am I going to get my pull in less than three weeks and beat Haley if I spend all my time watching stupid videos? I watch, and my mind wanders.

After what feels like way too long, Mr. Foster says, "Okay," and clicks off the video. "Now we can talk about Benderball."

Finally. We turn to face the class. Mr. Foster pulls one of the balls across the mat and hands it to me. It can't weigh more than half a pound.

"The goal of Benderball is to collect the most balls. It's that simple, and that difficult. In the beginning, it takes a great deal of concentration and strength of mind."

I watch a ball roll across the

mat toward Dawson, who frowns in concentration. Suddenly, the ball changes course and rises to Olivia, who's strapped into a harness hanging from the ceiling.

Dawson clenches and unclenches his hands, and the ball stops mid-rise. It wavers, suspended between them. Then it starts to rise toward Olivia again. It looks like she's won, until the bag on her shoulder slips off and all the balls she's already collected spill out.

"Hey!" she yells.

"That was good strategy from Dawson," Mr. Foster whispers. "Olivia didn't expect Dawson to pull on her bag instead of the ball."

"Oh, yeah! I thought her bag just fell off."

Mr. Foster smiles. "You have much to learn. For now, back to learning how to pull! First, you must spin a desire line."

He takes the benderball from me and sets it about three feet away. When he comes back to stand beside me, he leans in close. "The first thing you need to do," he whispers, sounding like a golf commentator on TV, "is be still. Empty your mind of distraction. Focus and concentrate. Imagine tiny particles floating all around us. They are called gravitons. I imagine them as a great puffy cloud of wool, like in the video."

"Okay, gravitons are like wool." I stare at the ball.

"Gravitons connect one thing to another, particle to particle. They fill the air between you and the things around you. Find the origin of your force within you. It will start in your chest, where the alignment medallion hung while you were aligned. Your force will spin the gravitons into a tight, thin thread of connection, just like the old woman spins the cloud of wool into a string of thread. We call that thread of connection a desire line."

Got it. Desire line.

"When pulling, the *connection* is the most important thing—not the object you are trying to pull. Once you find the line, apply constant pressure."

I stare harder at the ball. I one hundred percent *desire* to pull the benderball, but it doesn't move. Spinning wool is not how I imagined I'd get my superpowers, or whatever I'm supposed to call them. I hear Uncle Saul's voice in my head, telling me that I'm more powerful than anyone realizes. That I need to get my pull before the mysterious event coming up.

Mr. Foster's low, calm voice becomes distant as I concentrate on the benderball. Heat radiates from my heart, spreading to my chest and belly and face. It extends down the fronts of my arms and under my

finger- and toenails, but just like in the alignment chamber, my backside stays cool. I think I've found my desire line! I'll beat Haley's time and set a record for fastest to get a pull in the history of Gravitas!

I focus on my desire, like Mr. Foster said. I want the ball. Will get the ball. Get my pull before Haley. Be the best gravitar ever.

A pulse like the bang of a drum thrums inside me.

BAM!

Two yellow belts fall over and slide across the mat toward me.

SWOOSH!

Orange belts swing in their harnesses, as if a sudden gale has blown through the studio.

BOOM!

Dozens of benderballs hit my feet so hard that they sting. I bend over to shove off the benderball that's lodged on my toe, and...

SPLAT!

It's every kid's worst nightmare, throwing up in class. But at least I got my pull.

The heat quickly drains from the front of my body, and I feel limp like a rag doll. My knees buckle and I almost fall.

"Is everyone all right?" Mr. Foster sounds panicked. "Orange belts, come down."

The orange belts slowly descend in their harnesses. The whole class stares at me, shock written on their faces.

"That was the biggest yank I've ever seen!" says Annie. She wrinkles her freckled nose like she smells something bad… which, I guess, she does. The smell of my puke kind of makes me want to throw up again.

"That's enough, Annie. Most of you have yanked at some point. Dawson, grab some towels. Noah, are you okay?"

I still feel a bit woozy, but I'm more concerned about what I did wrong. "What's a yank?" I ask.

"A yank is chaotic," says Mr. Foster. "It's an uncontrolled tidal wave of a pull. It happens when you lose focus on the connection and your emotions spin out of control. This results in yanking multiple random items instead of just your target. Usually, it's just items that are very close to whatever object you're trying to pull, but in your case"—he glances around the room—"it seems you've pulled everything that was in front of you." Mr. Foster looks down at the mess on the mat. "Yanking also causes nausea, though actually throwing up only happens in rare cases."

I look at the balls clustered in the middle of the mat. It looks like Uncle Saul was right, and I *am* more powerful than other gravitars. But the look on Mr. Foster's face makes it clear that he doesn't see my yanking as a sign of greatness. "At least I used my powers, right?"

"It's no good using your powers if you can't control them. In fact, it's dangerous. A pull is controlled. A yank is not. Yes, you channeled an astonishing amount of power, but look at the result." Mr. Foster looks at me with worry in his eyes. "Whether it's a benderball or a bullet in the field, you must control your

emotions and focus fully on one strong desire line. Fear, anger, frustration—they can all cause you to get distracted."

"But I wasn't feeling any of those things!" I say.

Mr. Foster rubs a hand across his face, then says, "Don't worry, Noah." He sounds like he's trying to reassure himself rather than me. "Most gravitars yank in the beginning. Gravitar students are expressly forbidden from using their powers outside of class for this very reason. As long as a yank happens in the privacy of our studio, there's no harm done. Just a mess to clean up sometimes." He keeps his voice cheery and upbeat, but I can tell it's an act. "Class, please pack up, and then you're dismissed."

Mr. Foster leaves the studio as we start scooping up benderballs.

"Have *you* ever yanked?" I ask Olivia. She's the only one in class who's tried to be friendly so far.

"Not like that!" Dawson butts in. "Nobody here has." He looks at me like I'm a freak.

"When a gravitar yanks," says Luis, "it's like an air biscuit. A butt belch."

"Yeah, it's like a gravitar's way of farting." Annie giggles. "And that was the biggest, most powerful yank I've ever seen."

"It's not funny," says Olivia. "Mr. Foster was right. It's dangerous. But I'm sure it won't happen again, Noah." She gives me a quick smile and grabs her stuff.

"I hope not," says Dawson. "I've never yank-yacked. That was disgusting."

I hate to agree with Dawson, but he's right. It was disgusting. I was hoping to make an impression, but this wasn't what I had in mind.

Three weeks later, I still don't have my pull.

I had hoped to get it faster than Haley, but now I just hope I get it before two months is up, like a normal beginner Gravitas student. After everything Uncle Saul said, I can't believe I'm actually hoping for normal.

At least Mr. Foster found some karate pants that fit me, and I'm doing so well in basketball that Coach says I'll be a starter at our first game. And it's Halloween: the one night when the whole world is dressing up and pretending and nobody thinks it's weird.

Every year, Rodney, Haley, and I go trick-or-treating together. The last couple of years, the Fosters have asked us to take Brady: the perfect excuse to continue our tradition as long as we want. I've just finished putting on my costume—jeans, a white button-down shirt, a red tie, and a black vest—when Rodney gets to my house. He's dressed up like Dizzy Gillespie—big surprise. That's who he's been the past two years.

He hands me the glasses I asked to borrow: dark-framed with no prescription, just like the ones he's wearing. Perfect nerd glasses.

"Who are you supposed to be?" Rodney asks.

"Peter Parker!" I dig into my pocket and pull out a fake spider. "But not for long!"

Rodney fake-screams, and I chase him around my room. He pulls out his trumpet mouthpiece and starts blowing on it like a siren as he runs.

"Boys!" Mom calls. "You'd better go get Brady and Haley. I already had some kids ring the doorbell."

"Let's go!" I yell, and we race down the sidewalk to Haley's house. I *knock, knock-knock-knock, knock* on the door, and then we both walk in without waiting for a response.

Haley is standing in the foyer. She's wearing her regular clothes, but her hair is flowing down her back instead of pulled back in a ponytail, and it looks like she might be wearing some makeup.

"Who are you?" I ask.

"I'm Haley."

"Duh. I mean, who are you dressed up as?" I ask.

She glares at me. "Nobody! This isn't a costume, Noah."

"Ooh," says Rodney. "Smooth move, Noah."

Brady comes running down the hall in a green muscle suit with a black cape and a round red, white, and blue shield. Classic superhero mash-up.

"I'm a super, super, *super*hero!" he sings and strikes a pose.

"You look great, Brady!" I turn to Haley. "You better hurry up and get on your costume. People are already out, and we're going to miss all the good candy if we wait much longer."

"Um." She looks down, then back up at us. "I'm not going trick-or-treating. I'm going to a party... at Andy's house."

My stomach flips, like I just went around the loop on the Shock Wave roller coaster at Six Flags. "You're *what*?" I yell.

"It's no big deal. Weren't you invited? He said he invited the whole A team."

"Yeah, I was. And I said no. Because I always go trick-or-treating with my two best friends."

"Hey, *I* wasn't invited," says Rodney.

"Sorry, Rodney." Haley looks at me again. "You told Andy you were going trick-or-treating?" she asks, eyebrows raised.

"No. I told him I was taking *Brady* trick-or-treating. I can't believe you're ditching us for a party and you're just now telling us."

"He just asked me today, after school. I figured you were going too. Mom said she was going to take Brady trick-or-treating."

"But I want to go with Noah and Rodney," says Brady. "Let's go!"

"Yeah, let's go," says Rodney, pulling my arm. "We'll have fun. It's fine."

It's no good arguing with Haley now. She chose Andy over us, period. I turn and follow Brady and Rodney out the front door, grabbing a big fistful of candy from the Fosters' bowl on my way out.

"Real mature, Noah," Haley yells after us, then slams the door.

I try not to think about Haley having fun at Andy's party as we run from house to house, filling up our candy sacks, but it's hard to be ditched.

"Hey, Rodney. Do you think this is our last year to trick-or-treat?" I ask.

"Maybe."

I take a deep breath and let it go. "Fine. Then let's make it the best year yet!"

We visit every house in a three-block radius, continuing until our candy bags are stuffed. Haley can't possibly be having as much fun as we are.

Brady finally runs out of steam, so I give him a piggyback ride home.

Rodney spends the night at my house, and we stay up late, eating way too much candy. When we finally go to bed, I have a hard time falling asleep, but Rodney is snoring within minutes. *What if Haley is right?* I wonder. *What if I am immature? Maybe that's why I can't get my pull.* I get out of bed and pick up my newest snow globe. Uncle Saul says I have unbelievable powers, but I'm beginning to think that's about as likely as me shooting webs out of my wrist.

Wait a second.

I hold my arms out and bend back my hands, then imagine long lines of webbing shooting from my wrists. I used to do this all the time when I was a kid, and it sure makes more sense to me than spinning wool.

I can't wait to try it in class.

When Mr. Foster gives me a benderball on Wednesday, I don't even look at what the other students are doing. I set the ball down in a corner, then take a few steps back and close my eyes. I bend back my hands, exposing my wrists. I thrust out my chest, too, since that's where I'm supposed to be pulling from. Instead of imagining a web shooting out, I imagine gravitons floating in the space between the ball and me. I'm sure I sense them spinning into a long thread, hooking the ball, reeling it, and then—

Olivia screams.

What did I do this time? I spin around to see her swinging in her harness inches from the ground.

"Sorry, everybody. I was trying to slug and thought I had it, but then I fell fast."

"That's okay, Olivia," says Mr. Foster. "Back to your drills, everyone!"

What if it wasn't Olivia's fault? What if I did something wrong? I go back to bending my hands and thrusting out my chest, imagining webs, but when I think I'm getting close, I worry that I'm about to yank and so I stop. At the end of class, I still haven't found my desire line.

"Be patient, Noah," says Mr. Foster once it's just the two of us. "It takes time, and it does no good to get frustrated. Everyone fails, just like Olivia did today. It's part of the process."

"But what if I yank again? What if I really hurt someone this time?"

Mr. Foster shakes his head. "You can't be timid or fearful. That's a distraction." He glances at his watch. "If you have a few minutes, I want to show you something."

"Sure, what is it?"

"Come with me," he says and then begins to rise into the air. I feel a tug on the back of my neck, and slowly, I rise too.

"Whoa!" I spin beneath Mr. Foster like a bug dangling from a spider's thread. Moving makes me spin more, so I hold still.

It's amazing to be off the ground like this. I look up just as Mr. Foster reaches the bell on the ceiling, takes a card out of his pocket, and swipes it through a scanner on the side of the bell. A section of mirror in the front corner of the room swings up, revealing an opening. Dim light filters through, and I can hear people talking from the other side.

"Where are we going?"

"You'll see." Mr. Foster moves us forward until I'm practically face-to-face with my reflection in the mirror. He steps through the small doorway, and I reach up to pull myself in after him. Once I stand up, the door seals shut behind us.

When my eyes adjust, I can see that we're on a small landing, looking down at a huge, windowless room that's about as long as a football field. A catwalk below circles the perimeter, and what look like Hula-Hoops of various sizes hang from the ceiling, faintly glowing. The room is lit closer to the floor by lights mounted to the walls, revealing a full-size helicopter suspended just above the floor by big cables, a steep hill made of glass, and a pool of murky gray liquid. There's also a group of students in black belts milling about, chattering excitedly. They look older than me, maybe high schoolers, and their belts aren't just black. Some have a red horizontal stripe running through the black, and a few have a gray one.

"Why do their belts look different?"

"In your final three years of class, after you've earned black belt status, the stripe indicates your level. Gray is for the most advanced gravitars." Mr. Foster starts down some metal stairs. "Stay close." Our feet clang as we make our way down two flights and stop on the catwalk. We're still at least two stories above the floor, but I'm sure this whole room is underground.

"This is where the intermediate and advanced classes train and test. The whole facility is located under the office building next to the karate studio. It's all top secret, of course. Students and instructors have to use an ID card like this to be allowed entry."

Mr. Foster pulls the card he swiped earlier out of his pocket. "Watch what happens when I give it a gentle pull." A tiny emblem of the earth rises to the surface, the blue marble swirled with white clouds obscuring his name and rank. "The earth is the Gravitas symbol. Gravitars know no borders when it comes to using our powers. We'll go anywhere on earth to protect and defend all that is true, good, and beautiful. You'll receive your ID when you graduate to intermediate."

If I get that far.

"We're here to watch Phillip, a former student of mine, take his field agent test for the third time. He's that one there." He points to a tall student pacing nervously. "The test is so difficult that Gravitas gives candidates three chances to pass."

"If they fail three times, then they're suppressed?" I ask, my stomach churning the way it did when Wolfshaw first told me about suppression.

"Not necessarily. They'll have two choices: either work for Gravitas in another capacity, as an administrator or scientist or even an instructor like me—"

"*You* failed your test?"

"No. Not all teachers failed their test. I was an agent and then chose to be an instructor."

"Why would you choose to teach a class full of beginners when you could be out there saving the world?" I ask.

Mr. Foster smiles. "I had Haley, and then Brady. Two perfectly good reasons to stay close to home. And I haven't stopped saving the world. I just do it through students now. It was worth it. But as I was saying, a gravitar has two options if they fail their test. If they don't want to work for Gravitas, they can opt for voluntary suppression."

Voluntary? "Who would choose that?"

"Phillip."

I look down at the boy wearing a black belt with a gray stripe, surrounded by his friends. "Why?" I can't imagine choosing to be suppressed.

Mr. Foster shrugs. "He's decided he'd rather forget he has these abilities than not get to live out his dream of being an agent. In a lot of ways, you remind me of him, Noah. Both of you are dreamers. And his powers haven't come easy for him. I think it took him almost four months to earn his yellow belt, but he persevered, and here he is, a black belt. So don't give up! You have plenty of time to get your pull."

"Yeah, I guess you're right."

"And Phillip is even testing early!" says Mr. Foster.

"He is?"

Mr. Foster nods like a proud dad. "Phillip is eager to

begin basic training as an agent, but candidates can't do this until they graduate high school, so that's what he did. He took summer classes to graduate early, and that's why he's testing in December instead of in the spring like most students. His parents will be thrilled if their gifted and talented son gets recruited by the CIA right out of high school, even if they can't know exactly what he's doing."

So much for him being like me. If *he* struggles to pass this final test as a brainiac overachiever, what hope do I have?

"You'll have ten minutes to complete the course," a man's voice booms from below, and then a bell gongs. "Begin."

My stomach twists. This is it. If Phillip fails, he gets suppressed.

He stands poised for action, his toes behind a black line, staring intently at the smooth, two-story glass hill. His classmates cheer and whistle as Phillip starts pulling the hill slowly across the floor toward himself.

"He's got to stay behind the line until he pulls the hill close enough to jump onto, or he gets a strike." Mr. Foster uses his golf-commentator voice. "That hill weighs over six hundred pounds. He's compressing gravitons, increasing his mass, so the hill moves instead of him. We call it a press. You'll learn how to do it in intermediate."

As soon as the hill gets close enough, Phillip leaps and begins to climb, his eyes focused on the top.

"It looks easy, but that surface is slick and slippery," says Mr. Foster. "He must pull on the hill strongly enough to keep from slipping, but not so strongly that he's unable to take a step. It requires control and concentration."

It sounds impossible, but maybe that's because I can't even pull a benderball yet. Phillip doesn't seem to be having any trouble.

Suddenly, an alarm sounds and the lights on the wall start blinking.

"What's going on?"

"A distraction. It's another reason I brought you here today. As a gravitar, you can't let anything disrupt your focus. Fear and timidity can be just as distracting as that alarm, causing you to look away from your goal. Phillip has struggled with this part of the test. With all his strengths, he's easily distracted."

Phillip continues to climb. He doesn't seem to notice the noise and blinking lights. When he gets to the top of the hill, he jumps off. But instead of dropping to the ground, he rises and tilts into a horizontal position, his hands in front of him in the classic Superman pose. He begins to swoop through the hoops I noticed earlier, one after the other.

INCREDIBLE!

This is what I've been dreaming of my whole life.

"It looks like he's flying!" Is this what Uncle Saul meant when he said that I could soar?

"Maybe so. But remember, gravitars don't fly. It's a

complicated precision maneuver that requires pushing off the floor and pulling on the far wall at the same time. Combining a push and a pull is one of the last skills a gravitar learns in the second advanced class."

"Why does he have to push? Why can't he just pull on the ceiling?"

"Look up." Mr. Foster points out a series of panels suspended above the hoops, each hanging by a thin string from the ceiling. "If he pulls on those panels, they'll break free, and that's a strike. So he must use the floor and wall instead. It simulates being outside, where there's nothing above you to pull on. Navigating through the hoops proves he's capable of avoiding obstacles above street level in urban situations."

Phillip goes through the last hoop and begins to descend.

"Next, he'll slug to that tiny platform in the middle of the pool, which is filled with wet concrete."

So that's what the gray muck is.

"If he doesn't land just right, it'll be a strike and will make the rest of his test more challenging."

"You've got this, Phillip," I whisper, kneeling on the catwalk and hanging on to the rail.

When Phillip is almost down, a dog races across the course, barking. A buzzer sounds, and the booming voice calls out, "Strike one."

I look away from the dog and back at Phillip, who's standing knee-deep in the wet concrete.

Mr. Foster sighs. "That's Phillip's dog—a tough thing to ignore. Now he's got his first strike *and* the added weight of wet concrete on his pants."

"Gravitas brought in his *dog* for the test? That doesn't seem fair."

"It's imperative for a field agent to stay focused, no matter what. Any distraction can be the difference between life and death."

"Two minutes, thirty seconds remaining," the voice over the loudspeaker booms.

If Phillip is nervous or frustrated, his face doesn't show it. He simply looks up and soars back into the air. The buzzer sounds again, and the voice says, "Strike two."

"What happened now?" I ask.

"He forgot to stand on the platform. A candidate must do this before moving on."

That seems like a small technicality, and super unfair.

Phillip is now halfway between the floor and the catwalk, hanging on to the waistband of his pants with one hand, a grim but determined look on his face. His concrete-covered pants drip, looking heavy and cumbersome.

"Is he almost finished?" I ask.

"He's got to get up to the ceiling and ring the bell, then come back down for his final task."

"Bombs away!" yells Phillip suddenly. He lets go of his waistband.

His pants plummet to the floor, revealing boxer shorts with a picture of his dog on the butt. I can't help the laugh that explodes out of me. I'm glad I remind Mr. Foster of him. I *want* to be like him—bold and unafraid.

Without his pants, Phillip shoots to the ceiling quickly and rings the bell. Then he begins to slug down to the floor. It's a controlled descent, a slow-let-go, and I will him to move faster as the next time call sounds. "One minute, fifteen seconds."

"What does he have to do now?"

"Push the helicopter up and hold it for thirty seconds. He'll need to use a much heavier push than before." Mr. Foster leans forward. He looks nervous.

My pulse races. It sounds like the hardest task was saved for the end, and he's already got two strikes. But Phillip still looks

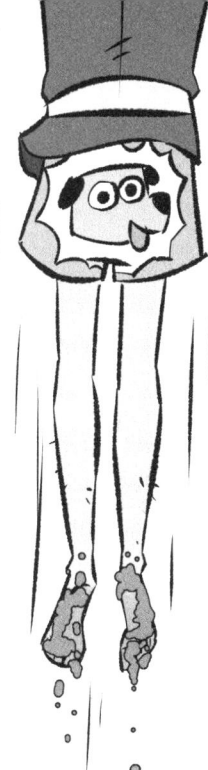

strong. Focused. As soon as his feet hit the mat, he rushes to the helicopter and kneels in the small gap underneath it. He stares at its belly, and slowly, the helicopter rises. I count along as the voice announces the final seconds… "Twenty-eight, twenty-nine, thirty!"

Phillip falls to his knees, and the helicopter drops rapidly. The cables creak with the force but keep it from crushing him. A buzzer sounds, indicating the end of the test, and Phillip's classmates rush to him as he crawls out from under the helicopter.

"You did it! Wahoo!" The yells and screams fill the arena, echoing off the walls.

"He did it!" I say, joining in from up high. I wish I could be down on the floor with the rest of them. Everything that's bothered me over the past few weeks—not getting my pull, yanking, being Haley's assignment—vanishes in my jubilation. I can still make out Phillip in the midst of all the other students, and even from up here, I can tell he's smiling.

An instructor approaches the celebration and bows to Phillip, who bows back. I recognize him—he's the man I met on my first day in the studio, Mr. Foster's assistant. He removes Phillip's black-and-gray belt, then coils it up and hands it to him.

Another adult approaches, this one wearing a suit instead of a karate uniform. He also looks familiar…

"That's Director Wolfshaw!"

"One of our best agents," says Mr. Foster.

Wolfshaw stands across from Phillip, but he doesn't bow. He salutes, and Phillip salutes back. It's a clear passing of the baton, a change of status. Phillip has transitioned from gravitar student to gravitar agent.

"He'll begin basic training after the Christmas break," says Mr. Foster.

"Awesome."

Hope and determination ignite in me like fireworks. I'll do whatever it takes to follow in Phillip's footsteps, even if it means yanking and enduring utter humiliation again. I'll get my pull, earn all the belts, and maybe even test early like Phillip someday.

When I do, I'll make sure to remember to wear boxers, not briefs.

11

I'm still on a high the next day—even after a grueling basketball practice where Coach made us run laps. His parting words replay in my mind as I walk home: *"You gotta work on your skills outside of team practices. Otherwise you'll never get better!"* Maybe I should also be working on my pull outside of gravitar class.

I know it's against Gravitas regulations. It was one of the first rules Mr. Foster told me. But I figure that as long as I'm careful, nobody has to know. Surely Gravitas won't be upset if extra practice helps me get my pull. I can't be the only student ever to try.

I close my bedroom door and clear a corner of my room so there'll be nothing for me to accidentally yank on, putting a pile of dirty clothes and my beanbag chair on my bed. Only my comic is in front of me, and I make sure a trash can is nearby, just in case. I figure that since I'm spinning a desire line, maybe it will be easier if I'm pulling on something I actually desire and already have a connection to.

With my hands bent back in my web-shooting pose, I focus on my comic book. I stare and stare . . . and stare.

I start getting frustrated, but then I think I feel a slight tug.

Maybe.

Mr. Foster says not to be timid or fearful, and to control my emotions. I can't give up. Phillip didn't give up.

I take a deep breath and try not to worry about yanking. *There it is*. I think I can feel my desire line. Now I just need to Pull. The. Comic.

I grit my teeth and stretch out my neck. *Move. . . . Move. Just a little bit. An inch. MOVE!*

My comic flutters open and slides to my hand, but there's also a loud *thunk* against the outside wall

of my room. And a nauseous feeling in my stomach. I grab my trash can just in time.

"Noah!" Mom barges into my room. "What was that sound? Did something hit the house?" She rushes across my room to my window and peers outside. "It looks like someone uprooted all our flowers and threw our little garden gnome! Who would do that? We're lucky it didn't hit the window!"

Oops. I didn't think about clearing the space *outside* my wall.

"Are you okay?" Mom asks, finally noticing the pukey trash can. "Have you been eating too much Halloween candy?"

"Yeah. Yeah, I have," I say weakly. Thankfully, that's enough for Mom to shake her head and leave me alone.

I look down at the comic page open in front of me. Peter Parker is walking down a cable, moving like a spider along its web—no practice required.

Must be nice.

By the time our first basketball game rolls around on Saturday of the next week, I've been in gravitar training for five weeks and *still* don't have my pull. I can't wait to take my frustration out on the court. Maybe I can't pull a stupid benderball, but I can shoot and steal and block and be Rim Rock's MVP. My plan to be gifted and talented at something so everyone at school will know my name is finally going to pan out.

The stands are full of parents and students, including Rodney with his trumpet, sitting in the back row with some band kids. I am so ready to swoosh balls and hear the cheers.

My teammates press in on either side of me, sweaty bodies and warm breath trapped in our pregame huddle.

"It's the first game of the season," says Coach. "And the Rams will be a tough opponent. I want you boys to go out there and do your best. This is what you've been working for. I want to see some heart. Chuck, get us hyped!"

Chuck starts the traditional game chant quietly. "Rim Rock, Rim Rock…"

"Rim Rock," we join in, first low, then louder and louder until we're shouting, "Rim Rock!"

"Mustangs!" Chuck finishes the chant, raising his fist in the air.

"Mustangs!" we echo, raising our fists too.

Coach starts me at power forward. It's a big honor, and I plan to make him proud. But within the first three minutes, I make a bad pass, miss a layup, and commit two lane violations. Coach calls a time-out and benches me. So much for gifted and talented.

"You need to settle down, Noah, and do what you've been doing in practice."

I am so mad at myself for screwing up. I know I can play better than that.

When the ball is back in play, Andy scores, and Rodney plays a short little ditty as everyone celebrates. He's got one for when we score, another for when we're heading down the court, and a longer one he plays during time-outs. When the other team shoots free throws, Rodney stands up and plays loud, short, distracting blasts of noise. Not a song—more like his own version of cars honking in a traffic jam. At one point he even starts a wave.

It's entertaining and all, but it's hard for me to enjoy. The whole team is playing terribly. Andy is off, and Chuck seems rattled. By the end of the first half, I have lines imprinted on my thighs from sitting on the metal bleacher for so long, and we're down seven points, 22–15.

During halftime, Chuck grabs my shoulder. "That trumpet doofus is a friend of yours, isn't he?" he growls. "He's screwing with our game!"

Coach comes in, and the locker room goes silent as I try to figure out what to do about Rodney.

"Noah, I'm moving you to center!" bellows Coach, startling me. I've got to forget about Rodney. Try to focus. "They're killing us on rebounds. Get in there and use your size."

"Yes, Coach!" I can do this. I won't let my team down.

"You boys play smart, or we're going to lose this game," says Coach.

"Yeah," Chuck says and jabs me with his elbow. "Play smart, and that trumpet kid better shut up."

My heart is pounding as I run onto the shiny wooden court. I say a little prayer and focus on keeping my breathing steady and calm, but it's hard with so much energy buzzing around me in the stands and on the court. Everyone is hyped.

The ref blows his whistle. We have possession, and Andy dribbles down the wide-open court, but his shot clangs off the rim. I miss the rebound, and I hear Coach yelling as I race after the ball. The Rams take a shot, but I block it and dribble back down the court, weaving around two defenders and going for a layup. Rodney is playing an inspiring song that amps me up, but at the last second, a Ram slaps at my hand and

I miss the shot. Thankfully, the ref blows his whistle and calls a shooting foul.

WAA-WAAAAAH! Rodney's trumpet blares.

I glance up into the stands as Rodney pounds his chest twice with his fist and then points at me like he's got my back. He's not going to let anyone foul his friend without doing something about it, and I appreciate that—but from the scowl on Chuck's face, it's clear that he doesn't. I catch Rodney's eye and shake my head slightly, hoping he gets the message, then walk to the free throw line.

It's just me, the ball, and the basket. I can't be timid or fearful if I'm going to make this shot. I bend my knees, take a deep breath, focus, and shoot. It drops neatly through the net, and the crowd cheers.

Rodney's trumpet joins in with a *duh-duh-DUH!*

The ref throws me the ball for my second shot. I bring the score to 22–17.

Rodney begins playing "We Will Rock You," and the fans start clapping and stomping on the bleachers. Within minutes, I manage to steal the ball and sink a three-pointer. The crowd goes wild as the score changes to 22–20. If I can do that again, we'll be ahead. What can I say? Being a hero is addictive.

The Rams fight back but quickly commit another foul, this time on Andy. His first shot is short and bounces off the rim. As he prepares to take his second shot, I can practically hear the fans holding their breath. Andy has the best free throw record on the team, but somehow he misses his second shot. He's *definitely* not on his game. Apparently, neither am I, since, once again, I miss the rebound. A Rams player snags it and makes his way down the court.

A cloud of frustration whips through me, fast and furious like a storm, a forest fire, a hurricane, a tornado. I chase the Ram down the court. I want—no, I *need*—to feel the ball against my palms, the tiny bumps against my fingertips.

If I can just get it back, I can make up for my earlier mistakes.

I can be the hero.

This must be what a desire line feels like, wanting something this bad. Without thinking, I try to pull on the ball.

THUD!

A cooler full of ice and Gatorade hits the court so hard that I feel it in my feet.

CRACK!

The flagpole falls and breaks, leaving the American flag resting on the shiny wood.

THUD!

Players fall face down on the court, which is littered with hundreds of paper cups and a spreading pool of blue Gatorade. Screams and shouts roar in my ears, and I double over, trying to catch my breath and keep myself from puking.

I yanked. Big time. In public.

I feel something tap against my foot and open my eyes. It's the ball I wanted with everything inside me.

My stomach clenches.

SPLAT!

I hurry to the locker room, desperate to get away from the mess I made. Dad comes rushing in after me.

"Are you okay?" he asks.

"Yeah, I'm fine. I don't know what happened out there." That's not true; I know exactly what happened out there, and I'll probably be suppressed by morning, but I can't tell Dad.

"They want everyone out of the gym. We need to go."

"They canceled the game?"

"Yeah, it will be rescheduled. Let's go, buddy."

I grab my gym bag and follow Dad outside. Coach has gathered the team in a huddle at the side of the parking lot. I want to join them, feel a part of the team.

"I'll meet you and Mom at home. I can walk," I tell Dad. He doesn't object.

But as I trot toward the team, they break. There's no "Three, two, one, Mustangs!" And nobody is smiling as they scatter. Chuck makes a beeline for me.

"Game's canceled, and Coach told us to go home. I bet we could have kept playing if you hadn't yacked on the court," The Tormentor says, sneering. "And if you don't tell your friend to stop blowing his stupid horn at our games, I'll make sure he can't."

Before I can figure out how to respond, he lumbers off. My phone buzzes.

RODNEY

> You okay hurl-meister?

I don't reply to Rodney's text. I text Haley instead.

NOAH

> meet me on the playground

HALEY

> see you there.

The park is buzzing with kids, and our usual spot on the robot slide is out of the question. So Haley and I snake through groves of cedar trees, where it's more private.

"Are they going to suppress everybody that saw what

happened?" What if they suppress my parents? Brady? Rodney?

"Shh. I bet they'll circulate some sort of excuse for what happened. They've done that before when there's a lot of people involved. But I bet Gravitas won't want you playing basketball again until you get your pull."

"What about me? Do you think *I'll* get suppressed?"

"I don't think so," she whispers. "You didn't do it on purpose."

Of course I didn't yank on purpose. But in those tense seconds, I wasn't feeling timid or scared, and I thought I'd finally figured out how to spin my desire line, so I tried to pull. On purpose.

Haley keeps talking. "Plus, if they suppress you, they'll never know why your yank is so powerful, and I think they're curious."

I picture an interrogation room filled with Gravitas agents and wonder how long I can keep quiet about Uncle Saul's visit.

"*I* wonder why your yank is so powerful. That was the biggest one I've ever seen. Dad said it had to take a huge amount of power to yank like that, and the one from class sounded pretty bad too. Maybe something *did* happen the night Saul dropped you."

It absolutely did, but I'm beginning to wonder if it was good or bad. "What if my uncle broke my powers when he dropped me and I'll never be able to pull?"

"You just have to be patient with yourself. If you can take whatever power you just used on the court and pull with it, that will be incredible!"

But I'm losing hope. I don't just feel like a screwup; I feel dangerous, out of control. If this is the extraordinary power Uncle Saul is talking about, I'm not sure I want it.

"Have you ever tried wiggling your ears?" Haley asks.

"What?"

"It may sound silly"—she blushes a little—"but that's how I got my pull. It took me months to learn how to wiggle my ears, feeling around for that muscle. When I was trying to get my pull, I did the same thing—feeling around inside myself until I got it."

Only Haley would spend months learning how to wiggle her ears, never giving up until she mastered it. I never learned how to wiggle mine, so that won't work for me, but all I say is "Thanks, Haley."

"Sure. One more thing. Word is sure to get out about what happened at the game. A yank that big will definitely be interesting to Saul. Be careful, and let Gravitas know if you see anything suspicious."

"I will." It's not a total lie. If I get suspicious about Uncle Saul and doubt whether I can trust him, I'll say something. I just wish he'd hurry up so I can ask him about what's going on with me. What if I'm not super powerful... just super messed up?

The next afternoon, Dad asks, "Remember how we used to go fishing?"

"Huh?"

He puts his hands behind his head and leans back in his chair at the kitchen table. "There's nothing like fishing to help you forget your troubles for a while."

I guess it's pretty obvious that I'm not over last night's game, and even though Haley doesn't think anyone will be suppressed, I'm still nervous about it.

"We may not be able to go fishing today, but I was thinking maybe you and I could practice casting in the backyard with the poles and weights and everything. Maybe it will help take your mind off things."

"Maybe."

I doubt it. I've never liked fishing like Dad does, but I appreciate him trying to help me forget about barfing in front of the entire school.

In less than an hour, Dad has created a whole setup in the backyard. He's put a bunch of targets at various distances from the back porch and already has small yellow weights tied to the ends of our lines. I cast first, and my line flies through the air. It kind of reminds me of a spiderweb shooting from a wrist and sailing to its target—but then it tangles and falls short.

Not surprising. Same thing happened when I was little.

"You've got to make sure you don't have any slack in the line before you cast." Dad helps me untangle it.

He hands the rod back, and I try again, making sure the line is taut first, but this time, I completely overshoot the target.

"Don't worry. You'll get it."

I sigh, tired of being told to be patient and tired of failing. I reel my line back in, dragging the weight across the grass... but this time, the light tension on my line catches my attention. What if this is what it feels like to pull a desire line? Mr. Foster told me I needed to find my own way to the pull. Pretending to shoot a web from my wrist or

spin wool didn't work, but maybe thinking of it like casting my line to hit a target could work.

I'm instantly a lot more excited, and Dad and I cast and reel, cast and reel, all afternoon. I get more accurate with hitting the targets, and each time I reel my line back in, I focus on the tug of the line, trying to memorize and absorb the feel.

"I'm glad this is helping you feel better."

"Me too."

He thinks he just found a way to cheer me up. He has no idea that this may be the key to so much more. Maybe at my next class, I'll go fishing for benderballs and catch one.

I get to school super early the next day and look for Rodney. I need to warn him that The Tormentor is going to come after him if he doesn't stop with the trumpet at our games. I think he'll listen better if I say it in person. He often comes to school early since his mom forbids practicing until she's on her second cup of coffee.

The band hall is like a cave, with high ceilings and no windows. I'm hit with its distinct smell—I suspect it's part spit. I walk by the shelf that holds all the trophies the band has won over the years, then walk down the skinny hall of practice rooms. They're partially soundproofed, but as I get closer to the end of the hall, I can hear a trumpet playing faintly in the last room. I look through the window on the door and find Rodney, who beckons me in.

"Are you practicing for our next game?" I ask.

"Nah, this is just for me, bro."

Rodney closes his eyes and resumes playing. His foot taps and his body sways. He isn't reading music—he's just playing whatever notes bubble up from somewhere inside him. He makes it look easy.

I wish getting my pull came as natural to me as music comes to Rodney. "I bet you're better than your dad was at your age."

Rodney lowers his trumpet and scowls. "Dude, why'd you have to kill my buzz?"

His parents got divorced years ago, and he still hasn't forgiven his dad for basically deserting their family and moving to New York to become a famous jazz musician. He doesn't even like to talk about him.

"Sorry. I just meant you're really good." I swallow. "*I love* to listen to you play, but maybe you shouldn't bring your trumpet to the games anymore. It made Chuck really mad."

"You know what I have to say to that?" asks Rodney.

"What?"

He brings his trumpet back to his lips and plays a

flubbery noise that sounds like the biggest butt belch I've ever heard. I bust out laughing, so he keeps doing it. He's obviously not worried about The Tormentor.

What else can I do?

I warned him, but Rodney is going to be Rodney: best butt-belching friend around.

That Monday is rough. I have a new nickname at school: the Basketball Barfer. I'm pretty sure Chuck started it.

Mom has a snack and a letter waiting for me on the table when I get home that afternoon. The letter's from Grandmother. She sends me one every month or so.

"It looks like your grandmother got a new seal," Mom says.

She always seals her envelopes with an *M*—for Minor—pressed into red wax. But this time there's a circle pressed into the wax, pocked with a few irregular spots.

Wait . . . those aren't spots. They're craters.

It's a full moon.

This letter isn't from Grandmother. It's from Uncle Saul.

I look up quickly, but Mom is looking at her phone and isn't really paying attention.

I break the seal and open the letter, my hands shaking a little. Everything about the letter looks just like Grandmother sent it: The envelope has her address on it, and the note is typed on a single sheet, in the same font she always uses.

> Dear Noah,
> I bought a new wax seal kit at a stationery store on 5th Ave. Hope you like it! I heard about the basketball game. I'm sorry you got sick, but it wasn't your fault. Remember that. It wasn't your fault! You did great, and I'm proud of you. I'll see you when you come for Thanksgiving!
> Love,
> Grandmother

It's a pretty basic letter, nothing special. But my uncle's message is clear. He knows about the yank, but he isn't worried like Mr. Foster and Gravitas are. And it sounds like he'll be in New York for Thanksgiving! That's just a week and a half away!

Maybe I'll finally find out about this mysterious event and how it can make me more powerful than any other gravitar. It can't come soon enough. But I remember that Uncle Saul said I needed to get my pull. Maybe he's not coming back until I do. If so, the yank is proof I'm not ready yet.

I resolve that this will be my day. If thinking about fishing doesn't work, maybe I'll try wiggling my ears.

★★★

"Noah, can you come here for a moment and shut the door?" Mr. Foster calls from his office.

Uh-oh. This can't be good.

"Do you realize how serious your yank was?" he asks as soon as the door clicks shut.

"Yes, sir."

"I'm sure Saul has heard about it by now."

I try not to think about the note sitting on my desk, afraid that something will show on my face.

"He'll be very interested in how powerful it was," Mr. Foster continues. "I doubt he'll care that it was out of control. Saul *likes* out of control. And he isn't our only concern, of course. You could have exposed the entire program."

"I know, I know. I'm really sorry." I'm struck by the difference between how Uncle Saul feels about my yank and how Gravitas does. "But it wasn't my fault. I couldn't help it—"

Mr. Foster holds up a hand like he's blocking my words. "No excuses. You've got to control your emotions no matter the situation, and you need to take responsibility for your actions."

"I know. I understand." His words remind me of my comic. *"With great power there must also come—great responsibility!"*

Mr. Foster picks up a small tube sitting on his desk. "We're going to practice opening these capsules in class today."

I guess the lecture is over. That wasn't too bad.

"Whenever Gravitas wants to save and protect information, they write it down and store it in one of these."

"Write it down, like, on *paper*?"

Mr. Foster nods. "Low-tech means hack-proof. Computer files can be hacked, but only a gravitar can open one of these capsules. Pulling or twisting with your hands won't work. Capsules with lower security clearance, like this one, can be opened by just one gravitar pulling, like this."

Mr. Foster stares at the capsule in his hand, and the lid pops off. He pulls out a rolled piece of paper.

"But the highest security level capsules, like the one Saul took, require four gravitars—two on each side—pulling at the same time. They also have a GPS that will activate as soon as they're opened."

"What's so valuable in the capsule my uncle stole?" I

ask, wondering if he'll tell me what Haley was unwilling to share. Wolfshaw said my uncle stole confidential information, and I'd like to know what it is.

"He stole the list of gravitars who were students the same year he dropped you from that balcony."

Huh. I had expected something more obviously top

secret, like the schematics to a Gravitas facility or something. "Why would Uncle Saul want that information?"

"That's a good question, and Gravitas doesn't have an answer. But if Saul opens that capsule, the identities of hundreds of agents could be compromised."

I look down at my white belt. I haven't even figured out how to pull a *benderball*. If the capsule he stole needs four gravitars to open, I can't understand why Gravitas is so worried about Uncle Saul coming to get me.

"I couldn't help him, even if he *does* ask me to help him open it. And he'd need two more gravitars, wouldn't he?"

"That's right." Mr. Foster hesitates, then says, "It's one of the reasons Gravitas didn't want to accept you into the program."

I bristle at his words, heat rising to my face. "What do you mean?"

"Sorry, Noah. But the way Gravitas saw it, if you didn't know any other gravitars, and if you were never aligned or trained, you'd be useless to Saul." He holds up the paper he took out of the small capsule. "This is a list of gravitars who weren't accepted into the program this fall. Your name could easily have been on it."

"Then why *did* Gravitas accept me as a student?"

Mr. Foster slides the piece of paper back into the

capsule and stares at it for a minute, then tests the cap to make sure it's sealed. "Because I convinced them that you will be an excellent asset to the program. And that if they want to catch Saul, you may be their best bet."

So they really *are* using me as bait. And it was Mr. Foster's idea! I try not to let my anger and disappointment show.

"One more thing. Saul is likely to reach out to you soon, so I talked to Gravitas about our family going to New York with you and your parents for Thanksgiving."

Oh no.

"It's the perfect opportunity for Saul to make contact and for us to catch him."

Yes, it is.

And I have the letter to prove it.

It's the first time I'm getting to participate in a full-class drill, and Mr. Foster pairs me with Dawson. Neither of us is happy about it, but we know better than to argue.

"I realize that you don't have your pull yet, Noah, but pulling on the lid of this low-level capsule and pulling on a benderball aren't all that different. Dawson, why don't you pull first and then give Noah a few minutes to try?"

"Yes, sir." Once Mr. Foster is out of earshot, he whispers, "I hear they call you the Basketball Barfer."

How did he hear that? I roll my eyes and act like I don't care. "Only the idiots do." He must be friends with someone from my school.

I hold the capsule with both arms extended. Dawson stares at it, and I have to tighten my grip against the tug. Seconds later, the cap pops off.

"Easy." Dawson stifles a yawn, but I can totally tell it's fake. "Now it's your turn."

I pass him the capsule, step back, and concentrate on staying calm, but it's hard with Dawson's smug smirk in view. I squint, blocking out everything but the silver lid of the capsule. I recall the feeling of casting my fishing line and imagine casting my invisible desire line in the same way. I feel something within me, like a weight landing on a target, and begin reeling my line back in. I slowly increase the force of my pull, remembering the weight on my fishing line dragging across the grass and making my desire line taut too.

POP!

The capsule hurtles toward my face, and I jump out of the way just in time. Dawson comes stumbling toward me, still holding the capsule.

"He yanked again!" Dawson yells.

He doesn't have to be so loud about it. I would be frustrated, but something felt different this time.

"Are you nauseous?" Mr. Foster asks.

"No." *That's* what's different. I may have yanked again, but thinking about fishing must have worked a little, because I'm not even a tiny bit sick.

Mr. Foster slowly nods, taking a quick look around. "Everything is still in place," he says softly.

"Except Dawson," I add. "I think I yanked him too." And it felt good.

"Noah . . . I don't think that was a yank." Mr. Foster hesitates, then goes on. "It was a pull. A strong one. So strong I'm guessing Dawson had to fight to hang on, which is why he stumbled toward you."

I notice the rest of the students have stopped practicing on their own capsules and are all staring at us, but I don't care. *This* seems worth the attention.

"Was it a *heavy* pull?" I ask. "Like, I could pull myself to the ceiling?"

I look up and begin to spin a line.

"Wait!" yells Mr. Foster, but it's too late. I'm reeling it in so fast that I zoom up.

SLAM!

And I black out.

When I wake up, the class is gone and I'm lying flat on the mat. My head hurts. A lot.

"What happened?" I ask softly.

"You pulled so hard you smashed your head on the ceiling," says Mr. Foster. "You're going to have to go to the doctor and make sure you don't have a concussion.

But if anyone asks, the official story is that you got kicked in the head."

It definitely *feels* like I got kicked in the head... but even with the pain, I'm happy.

I did it! I more than did it. Uncle Saul was right: I *am* powerful. My first time pulling, and it was a *heavy* pull.

"So I earn my yellow *and* my orange belts?" I ask.

"No, I'm sorry. That's not the way it works."

"What?" I lift my head too quickly and immediately have to lower it back down.

"This has never happened before. Gravitars always move through a predictable sequence, getting their pull before their heavy pull." Mr. Foster looks at me with worry in his eyes. "The average gravitar finds their power, their pull, and then works on strengthening it. But you... It's like you've got all this power stored up, and now that you've accessed it, I'm worried you can't control it."

I can't believe it. Now they don't trust me because I'm too powerful? I bet that if my uncle saw what I just did, he'd say I was **INCREDIBLE! AMAZING!** and *not* **OUT OF CONTROL!** I'm definitely ready for whatever big event Uncle Saul was talking about.

"You'll earn your yellow belt when you learn how to control that power," says Mr. Foster. "And then you can officially test for orange while wearing a harness. No more shooting to the ceiling without a plan."

"Yes, sir" is all I say, keeping my voice controlled just like Gravitas wants, hiding my frustration.

I raise my hand in class on Wednesday, excited to finally earn my yellow belt. "I'm ready to test," I say when Mr. Foster calls on me. He hands me a benderball, and I place it a few feet away from me. The class scatters so everyone is standing behind me. Not funny. I cast and spin my desire line and hook the benderball, no problem.

But when I pull, it comes flying at me so fast that I have to duck to avoid getting hit.

Someone yells, "Ow!" and I turn to see Olivia rubbing her arm where a red welt is already rising, pocked with white dots.

"I'm really sorry! I didn't mean to." Benderballs are as light as air. I can't believe it made a mark when it hit her. I wish I had hit Dawson instead.

Mr. Foster looks at me sharply, and I remember what he said about accepting responsibility.

"You must be able to pull the ball steadily, with

control, to earn your yellow belt. And next time, *you* take the hit, Noah."

I don't argue. I've hurt people with my power twice now—once with my yank at the game and now with my pull. I've got to do better, so I keep practicing. But each time, my pull is too strong. Even though those little balls sting like a wasp each time they hit, I don't move out of the way.

By the time class is over, I'm no closer to earning my yellow belt than I was when I started. I'm just bruised and sore, and a little scared that Gravitas is right. Maybe I really am out of control.

Five days after the game, everyone seems to have forgotten about me puking on the court . . . except for Chuck.

"Hey, Basketball Barfer," he says when I come into the locker room after school on Thursday. "I'm gonna call you B.B. for short."

I could pull him across the room if I wanted to, but I restrain myself.

Unfortunately, when we get on the court, I see Rodney on the back bleacher. I motion him down. "What are you doing here?" I whisper. "You don't want to set off The Tormentor."

"He said he didn't want me at games. This is practice!" Rodney says and smiles.

Coach blows his whistle, and I leave Rodney to join the team at midcourt.

"I asked the band director to send that kid to play

during practice"—Coach points into the stands—"so you boys can learn how to focus. You can't let yourselves get distracted."

"If your friend messes with my game, he's toast," Chuck says to me as we line up for drills. The Tormentor has definitely been awakened.

Ignore him, I tell myself.

Practice goes pretty well. At least for me. I miss only a few free throws, but Chuck is playing terribly. With each missed shot, bad pass, and fumble with the ball, Chuck glares into the bleachers, but Rodney doesn't seem to notice. He just keeps playing upbeat riffs—Rodney originals—when we make our shots and long low notes or flubbery farts when we mess up. They make some of the guys laugh but not Chuck.

At the end of practice, Rodney motions that he'll wait for me in the hallway. But as I make my way to the locker room, I see Chuck heading out the door across the gym—the same one Rodney went through. He's singing one of the songs Rodney was playing, except the words are a little bit different.

"I will, I will rock you."

That doesn't sound good.

I hurry after him and make it to the hall just in time to see Chuck at the other end, about to slam-dunk Rodney's trumpet into a trash can.

I don't hesitate. Nobody treats my friends like that

when I can do something about it. Not even The Tormentor, who is way heavier than me. He probably won't budge. I still have to try.

Laser-focused on Chuck, I yell, "Drop it!" I don't even try to control myself as I spin a desire line, and power bursts out of me in a heavy pull.

CLANG!

Chuck slams to the slick, hard floor and slides toward me, still holding Rodney's trumpet.

"Whoa. How did you do that?"

Shoot. Rodney just saw everything.

★★★

As we walk to my house, Rodney cradles his damaged trumpet like a baby. It's too bent to fit in his case, so I'm carrying that.

"Are you going to explain to me what happened back there?" he asks.

I still don't know exactly what happened. Technically, I shouldn't be able to pull somebody heavier than me until I learn how to press in intermediate. Maybe it's just more proof that I'm super powerful, like Uncle Saul said. "Wait until we're in my room," I tell Rodney.

If there's a rule about not practicing outside of gravitar training, I can only imagine how much trouble I'd be in if anyone found out that I purposefully used my powers on Chuck. He looked confused when we left the school, so I'm hoping he assumes he slipped or something. If he suspects something weird happened and talks, he'll have to rat on himself and explain why he had Rodney's trumpet in the first place. Now I just need to make it clear to Rodney that *he* can't tell anyone either.

Rodney looks at me with eyebrows raised. "You're making me nervous, bro. What are you afraid of?"

What am I afraid of? Suppression? Going back to the ordinary Noah Minor after getting a taste of the extraordinary?

"Spill it," says Rodney the moment we shut the door to my room.

"Do you remember the day we had vision testing?" I ask. And then I tell him about Wolfshaw and the eye test, about getting aligned, and Benderball, and how hard it's been to get my pull. I tell him how I yanked in class *and* at the basketball game and how I thought I might get suppressed, but I didn't.

As I talk, he fingers the valves of his dented trumpet like he's composing some sort of soundtrack. It's what he always does when he's nervous or excited.

When I tell him that Uncle Saul dropped me from the balcony on purpose and that he showed up in my kitchen, Rodney looks at the *New York Times* article on my wall and says, "I never trusted him."

"Really? Why?"

"Just look at him." Rodney points to the picture in the article. "Shifty eyes."

Umm, we have the same eyes. "Well, Uncle Saul says I'm incredibly gifted and that there's some big event coming up that will make me more powerful than even advanced gravitars."

"I don't care what he says. He dropped you off a balcony!"

"Yeah, but if it made me more powerful, it was worth it, right?" Rodney doesn't answer, and I decide not to tell him about my uncle's letter and how he's coming to

New York. He'd just worry. "Uncle Saul said that burst of adrenaline gave me superpowers. *Super* superpowers. I just have to learn how to control them. I actually got my pull this week. And not just a normal pull. My *heavy* pull. Mr. Foster said—"

I clap my hand over my mouth. I wasn't planning to tell him about Haley or Mr. Foster.

There's a bit of a silence as Rodney squints at me.

"Why does Mr. Foster know you're a gravitar?" His question is slow and drawn out with suspicion.

I've already told him so much. What's a little more? Besides, I know Rodney won't tell.

"Mr. Foster *is* a gravitar. He's my teacher. And..." I hesitate, then go ahead. "Haley is a gravitar too."

Rodney's mouth drops open, and he fingers his trumpet faster.

"Remember, you can't mention *any* of this to *anyone*!" I say. "If Haley knew I told you, she'd kill me before I ever got suppressed. I just wanted to tell you so you'd understand what's been going on between us. She's already in intermediate class because she got to start early. In fact, I've been her *assignment* for the last year. She's basically been watching me in case Uncle Saul comes back, and she's supposed to report to Gravitas if he does."

"Whoa! That's so messed up!"

"Right? That's why I was mad at her a while back, but we're cool now."

Rodney nods and then breaks into a huge smile. "I can't believe my two best friends are *superheroes*. Dude, you're living in a comic book! You just need to find some more bad guys now that you've taken care of The Tormentor."

"Well, I'm actually not supposed to use my powers outside of class. And what I really need to do is earn my yellow belt before Gravitas kicks me out of the program and suppresses me. You saw what happened with Chuck. I was only trying to pull your trumpet out of his hands, and instead, I dragged him halfway down the hall."

"And dented the heck out of my trumpet."

"Right. I've got to figure out how to control my pull. When I do, I'll earn my yellow belt."

"Now that I know about all of this, maybe I can help," Rodney says.

"Last time I practiced outside of class, I hit our house with the garden gnome. We're going to have to be careful."

"I got you." Rodney holds out a fist. I'm reaching over to give it a bump when the doorbell rings. I jump up, feeling panicky, which is stupid. It's not like whoever is at the door could hear us.

I hurry down the hall with Rodney right behind and see Haley standing on the porch.

"Hey, guys," she says when I open the door. "What's up?"

I glance at Rodney. His eyes are wide, and he's biting his lip. For the first time in his life, I think he's honestly afraid to speak.

"Nothing!" I say, filling the growing silence. "Um, we're just hanging out."

It's *technically* not a lie, but I can feel myself sweating as she stands there tapping her notebook with her fingers. Finally, she says, "Well, are you going to let me in?"

"Oh, yeah! Yeah. Come on in."

"Thanks." She walks past us, but it's clear my awkwardness has made her suspicious. As she heads toward my room, I feel uneasy—like the secrets I just spilled are lying around like dirty clothes. Rodney's silence doesn't help. He would normally have made some kind of lovey-dovey joke by now.

I look at him and cock my head in a way that I hope says, *Come on. Be your normal, loud, funny self.*

"Oh no, what happened to your trumpet, Rodney?" Haley asks. She picks it up off my floor.

Rodney looks at her and then down at the shiny black case.

What if he cracks? What if he says something about Chuck and Gravitas?

"It got dropped," he says.

Haley furrows her brow. "That's it? It got dropped. Did you drop it or did someone else? How did it happen?"

"I did!" Rodney says quickly. "Um, I slipped on a banana peel."

Really, Rodney? That's the best he could do?

"What's up with you guys?" asks Haley, looking back and forth between us. "You're acting weird."

"We're always weird," Rodney replies. He slips his mouthpiece out of his pocket and starts to blow, inflating his cheeks. Haley raises her eyebrows and looks at me, but I just shrug and smile.

She shakes her head. "Fine. Don't tell me." She sits at my desk and picks something up. "Oh! A new letter from your grandmother! What society event did she share about this time?" she asks.

I had days to put away my uncle's letter, but I never did. How could I have been so careless?

"It's just a note to say she can't wait to see me over

Thanksgiving." I hope Haley doesn't pick up on my nervousness. Uncle Saul didn't say anything to give himself away, but Haley has a nose for lies. Especially my lies.

"I'm so excited that we get to go to New York with your family this year!" says Haley, putting the note back down.

Phew.

"I can't wait to meet her!"

"*You're* going to New York with Noah?" asks Rodney, a smile developing on his lips. "Have y'all seen that movie *Sleepless in Seattle*? It's my mom's favorite. At the end, this couple meets at the Empire State Building on Valentine's Day and—"

"Rodney!" Haley and I yell. Everything seems to shift back to normal.

I have nothing to worry about.

Rodney comes home with me after school the next day. The plan is for him to spend the weekend helping me learn to control my pull.

"We'll have to be careful so Mom doesn't catch us," I say once we're in my room. She's baking Thanksgiving cookies, which means once they're cooled and iced, she's bound to bring us a few to sample.

"You have nothing to worry about!" says Rodney. "I'm just going to teach you how to play trumpet."

"You're what? What's that have to do with getting my pull?"

"Just listen." He unlatches his case and pulls out his loaner trumpet, lifts it to his lips, and plays a note. "That's a D." He plays the same note, but slightly higher, and then again, a little lower. "Those are all D. The first one was on key, the second was sharp, and the third was flat. I press the same valves, but the sound changes because of how I hold my lips."

Rodney takes his phone out of his pocket and opens an app. "This will play the perfect pitch for D."

He plays the note again, his fingers never moving. He starts out a little too high, then dips below the note, then slides to the tone that matches the app perfectly.

"Um, this is cool, but—" I start to say, but Rodney interrupts.

"It takes *control* to stay in tune, to match the note. You have to control your breathing and your lips. When everyone in band is in tune and we all hit the right pitch, it's like magic. Maybe if you learn how to match the pitch, you'll learn to have good control, and it'll help you pass the bendyball test."

"Bende*r*ball," I correct him.

"Whatever." He holds his trumpet out to me. "Playing the trumpet takes control and so does pulling. You've tried everything else, so what do you have to lose?"

I look down at the instrument. "Maybe." I had hoped for a better idea, but he's right. Gravitas training isn't helping, and I need to be able to control my pull before I see Uncle Saul. I take the trumpet from Rodney.

"First, you need to breathe."

"That, I can do. I've been doing it my whole life."

"The kind of breathing you need to play a good, strong note is different. You gotta pretend you're sucking the last little bit of a milkshake through a straw."

I purse my lips and suck hard.

"Now pretend you're blowing all that air into a balloon." He puts his hand on my belly. "Your breath comes from here. Now do it again. In like a straw, out like a balloon."

I breathe in and out, feeling a little ridiculous.

"Keep practicing," he says.

I breathe again and again, filling and emptying my lungs, until I start to feel lightheaded. And impatient. "Okay, what now?"

"Now you play D."

I put the trumpet to my lips, press the valves Rodney points out, and blow into the mouthpiece. It sounds terrible.

"Move your lips around!" He puts a finger on his lips and blows, tilting his lips slightly. I try to copy him, and the pitch swings up, then down, then up, then down.

Rodney turns up the volume on his phone so I can hear the note I'm supposed to hit. I close my eyes and focus on the sound. My pitch continues to swing around, not quite matching D, but I can tell I'm getting closer and closer, until finally... I match the note and play it just right. I open my eyes and look at Rodney in surprise, but he motions for me to keep going, so I keep blowing. Pretty soon, each time I try, I hit a perfect pitch.

"Excellent!" says Rodney, raising a fist in the air.

"How about you boys take a break from your trumpet lesson?" says Mom, coming in with a plate of cookies shaped like turkeys. Their iced feathers are covered with red, orange, and yellow sprinkles. They smell amazing. She places them on my desk and heads back to the kitchen. "Enjoy!"

Rodney picks up a turkey and takes a big bite. "Mmm, still warm." The icing sticks to his fingers, and the sprinkles crunch in his teeth.

"Let me have one." I reach for the plate, but Rodney holds it away from me.

"Hey!"

"Try to pull one while you're matching the pitch," he says. Then he hits D on the app.

Pulling already takes a lot of focus, and I can't get it right. Now I'm going to try while playing an instrument?

"Come on—trust me!" Rodney says. I give him the stink eye but bring the trumpet back to my lips. "No barfing," he warns.

"No promises." I pucker my lips, take a deep breath, and blow. I focus on matching the pitch first. It doesn't take long before I find it. I take another breath and keep playing. Each time, I match the note perfectly. Just me, D, and a plateful of cookies.

I train my eyes on one and picture all the gravitons floating around between us. I begin to gather them into an imaginary fishing line that I've cast to reel in the turkey. My focus on my breathing slips, and I play a sour note, but I quickly adjust and get back to playing pitch-perfect D. I continue playing and zero in on the cookie. Somewhere between my gut and my heart, there's a want, a need that thrums like a guitar string. **TWANG!** I can feel my desire line, but instead of a rushing force, it's more like Dad reeling in his fishing line, steady and controlled.

I begin to slowly pull on the invisible thread. It feels taut, like Dad's line, not tangled with a rush of emotions. The cookie begins to slide across the plate. I keep my pull controlled and steady, my breath twisting and curling and then somehow becoming D, and my big, empty self deeply inhaling to do it again.

And then the turkey cookie gently bumps my knee and stares up at me with his icing eyes.

Rodney throws his arms up in victory. "You did it!" he says, his voice quiet but excited.

I did. I finally found my way.

I don't feel a storm coursing through my body, don't feel spent, don't feel nauseous or out of control. I feel calm, proud, and hungry. I take a big bite.

"How do you feel?" asks Rodney.

"Powerful." I shove the rest of the cookie in my mouth, chew, and swallow.

Superhero powerful.

I spend all weekend practicing so I'll be ready to earn my yellow and orange belts in class and finally show Gravitas what I'm capable of. By Monday morning, I can spin a desire line in under two seconds.

I'm so controlled that I can pull a tiny piece of lint off Rodney's shirt without him even feeling it and so powerful that I can pull myself to my bedroom ceiling. No, I can't slug; therefore, when I stop pulling, I fall on my bed so hard I almost break the frame, but at least I planned ahead and had a soft spot to land. Mom comes running to find out what happened, and Rodney and I get in trouble for jumping on the bed.

When we're alone again, Rodney asks, "Now that you've got your powers, what's your superhero name going to be?"

I think for a minute. It's got to be good. I glance at

the *New York Times* article on my wall, and it hits me. "Same as it's always been. The Minor Miracle."

I'm on cloud nine as I walk into the school... until I see one of Haley's dance posters with the words "Starry, Starry" crossed out and "Barfy, Barfy" written instead. I rip it down but find another one, and another. They've all been messed up. When I see Haley, she's holding a pile of posters, too, and she's furious.

"Chuck is such an idiot!" she yells. "When I see him, I'm going to—"

"I'm not a fan of The Tormentor, but how do you know it was him?" I ask.

"He asked me to the dance, and when I told him no, he got all mad and told me I'd be sorry. He actually said nobody wants to go to our barfy, barfy dance anyways."

"He's such a lecherous loser! Are you going to tell the principal it was him?"

She rolls her eyes. "I'm not a snitch."

"Well, someone should make him pay." Haley doesn't respond, too busy counting how many posters she needs to replace.

Nobody messes with my friends. This time, I won't be as obvious as I was outside the gym, pulling Chuck down the hall. Now I'm The Minor Miracle, I'm in control, and he'll never know what happened.

★★★

"B.B.!" The Tormentor calls when I walk into the cafeteria a few hours later. "How's your dorkestra friend?"

"Shut up, Chuck."

He laughs at me, a wad of blue gum sitting on the middle of his tongue. If at any point I was doubting my plan, I'm full of resolve now. I can't let him treat people like this.

I head to my usual table, but I don't sit.

"I think I'm going to sit with the team today," I tell Rodney.

"Why?" he asks, glancing at the table where Chuck is laughing too loudly. "I thought you preferred to spend as little time as possible with... that."

I lean over and say in a low voice, "Just keep an eye on The Tormentor. And remember... it wasn't me."

His eyes get wide, and I give him a little nod before walking over and sitting at the table where most of the eighth graders on the A team congregate each day.

I place myself strategically across from Chuck, two people down. He's talking so loudly that his voice carries across half the cafeteria—quite a feat for a room full of a couple hundred kids chattering, laughing, squealing, burping, and yelling. But it's no problem for The Tormentor.

"She just about fainted when I asked her," Chuck is saying.

"Maybe you should have brushed your teeth first," says Andy, visibly irritated. I don't know how he can sit with Chuck every day. But I guess Andy has to tolerate him since he and Chuck are co-captains and Coach expects them to put on a unified front.

"What are y'all talking about?" I ask.

"Not that it's any of your business, B.B., but I got a date for the dance," Chuck says.

What a nattering nimrod. "Me too! I'm planning on going with Haley." And Rodney. But he doesn't need to know that.

Chuck sneers at her name. "Did you know it's in the gym?" he asks. "I hope you don't 'barfy, barfy' on the dance floor."

That gets a few laughs, but Andy, who's sitting next to him, says, "Don't tell me you're the one who messed up all those posters!"

Chuck shrugs and grins, making Andy shake his head. Even a good guy like Andy can't stop The Tormentor. That's why The Minor Miracle needs to step in and save the day.

I watch as Chuck dips his roll into brown gravy and

pops the whole thing in his mouth. Then, mouth still full, he shovels in some turkey and stuffing, creating a juicy wad of mush.

I focus on that mush. Blocking out the noise of the cafeteria, I gather gravitons into my desire line. When it's taut and ready, I set my hook inside Chuck's mouth and pull.

A hunk of food flies out of his mouth and **SCHLUP!** hits the table. The wet glob of bread, turkey, stuffing, and gravy skids to a stop a few inches from my lunch tray.

"Yeah, that's sick!"

"Nasty!"

"Keep your food in your mouth!"

The whole table echoes my disgust. Nailed it!

The Tormentor's face is flushed. "Why would I be jealous of you, twerp?"

"Because Haley said no when you asked her to the dance," I shoot back.

Chuck's face is now full-on red.

"You asked Haley to the dance?" asks Andy. This seems to upset him more than the partially chewed food flying out of Chuck's mouth.

"No! I mean, kind of, but I didn't mean it," says Chuck. "It was just a joke."

I want to look over at Rodney to see if he's enjoying this, but I don't. Instead, I glance to where Haley's sitting just a few tables away. The ruckus has caught her attention. Surely Ms. Rule Follower will be okay with a little revenge after what The Tormentor did to her posters.

Everyone at our table calms down, and Chuck takes another giant bite. This time, he keeps his mouth closed. But I'm not done messing with him.

"So, Chuck, who *are* you taking to the dance?" I ask.

He makes the mistake of not swallowing his food before he says, "Nicole Brando."

Several chunks of half-eaten food tumble out of his mouth and slide toward me again.

"Dude!"

"Disgusting!"

"Chuck, keep your food in your mouth or get out of here," says Andy. He takes his napkin, pinches one of Chuck's half-eaten bites off his tray, and tosses it into a trash can with a perfect swish.

Chuck doesn't respond and instead picks up his soda and takes a swig. This time, I concentrate on his nose and spin a new line. I can't see the liquid, so this is harder, but I'm The Minor Miracle. I can do this. I pull at his nostril, hopefully creating suction. Soda is the only thing I could possibly pull out of there, except maybe boogers, which would be equally disgusting. My bet pays off when a spray spews out of his nostrils.

"Ow!" yells Chuck. He shoots up and grabs a napkin, his chair clattering loudly to the floor.

Man, I'm good. The Tormentor is no match for The Minor Miracle.

The whole table is standing now, a few of the guys yelling at Chuck for splattering them with nose soda. The cafeteria erupts into all kinds of noise as people try to figure out what's going on.

When I look at Haley again, I see her jaw clench. I think she's figured out that this wasn't just Chuck being gross. She stands, pins me with a piercing stare that could only mean, *Follow me right now, or suffer the wrath of Haley Foster,* and walks out.

Uh-oh.

"Haley!" I call as I try to catch up with her.

She stops farther down the hall, her arms folded across her chest. It's obvious that she's fuming.

"I can't believe you did that," she whispers furiously as soon as I'm close enough to hear.

There are a few random students in the hall, but nobody is paying attention to us. Most are peering into the cafeteria, trying to see what's going on.

"We both know Chuck deserved it," I whisper back.

"It doesn't matter if he deserved it!" she hisses. "You can't pull in public! And how did you even learn how to do that? Last week you couldn't stop pelting yourself with benderballs."

I ignore her question. She'd be even more mad if she knew I was practicing outside of class. And if she knew about *Rodney*? I don't want to think about it. I just need to calm her down. "It was just a prank. And Chuck has no idea *I* was doing it."

"Gravitars don't do pranks." Her voice is still low, but this time there's a threatening edge to it, and I wonder if she's mad enough to tell Gravitas what happened.

"Please don't tell your dad." I hate to beg, but I have no choice. I can't get suppressed just when I've finally mastered my powers.

She glares at me. "I can't believe you did this." She spins on her heel and heads back to the cafeteria, holding my fate in her shaking hands.

Rodney's waiting at the door, and he says something to her. I can't hear what, but she looks from him to me, then back at him. She goes inside without a word.

I hurry over to Rodney.

"What did you say?" I ask.

"I just asked if you two were okay."

"You're sure that's all? You didn't say anything that would make her think you know something?"

Rodney puts a hand on my shoulder. "Relax. It's fine. She doesn't suspect a thing."

I look past Rodney into the cafeteria, where Haley is sitting at her table, watching us.

I hope he's right.

"What is the purpose of Gravitas?" Mr. Foster asks, starting class like he always does. He didn't pull me aside before class, so I guess Haley didn't tell her dad about what I did to Chuck at lunch. At least, not yet.

"To protect and defend all that is true, good, and beautiful!" we recite.

That's what I did today. I defended my friends, standing up for what is true. And it was a beautiful thing. Couldn't Haley see that?

As soon as we're done with warm-ups, Dawson and I raise our hands at the same time. Mr. Foster calls on Dawson first.

"I'd like to test for orange today, sir," he says.

"Very good, Dawson. I think you're ready. And, Noah?"

I smile and put down my hand. "I'd like to test for orange also."

"But you don't have your yellow belt yet," Dawson protests.

"I'd like to test for that too."

Mr. Foster raises his eyebrows. "Last time you were in class, you were still struggling to *control* your pull. You haven't been practicing outside of class, have you, Noah?"

I feel my cheeks get warm. "A little." I can't lie myself out of this. Even Haley knows I spent the last class pelting myself with benderballs.

Mr. Foster shakes his head, obviously disappointed in me. "You disobeyed a direct order, and besides, gravitars are only allowed to test for one belt at a time. You must show consistent mastery of a skill for two weeks before trying to move to the next level. You haven't even shown mastery of your pull for one *day*, so you certainly aren't ready to test for orange. And because you practiced at home, you won't be testing for any belt today, Noah."

Every eye in the class is watching me. I shift from foot to foot, embarrassed and frustrated with myself. The Minor Miracle should have known better. If I had kept my hand down and just "practiced" with a benderball during class, everyone would have marveled at how quickly I picked it up. I could have been the star student for once, instead of the problem child.

"I'm also going to have to ask you to wear a monitor," Mr. Foster continues.

He walks to the alignment closet, takes something out of one of the boxes, and comes back holding a ridiculous necklace. A charm the size of a quarter hangs from the silver chain, with the letters *BBKS,* for Black Belt Karate Studio, painted on it. It looks like something a five-year-old bought with tickets spit out of an arcade game.

"This will detect any disruption to gravity and notify Gravitas immediately." Mr. Foster slips it over my head and adjusts the length so the charm rests on my chest. "If you use your powers anywhere but here or take it off, we will know."

My heart sinks. It feels like I've just been leashed.

"I'll remove it after Thanksgiving, when I allow you to test for your yellow belt, and then you'll wait two more weeks to try for orange." He turns away from me. "Dawson, are you ready?"

Dawson hooks himself into a harness so he'll be caught if he fails and so he can get back down. Then he positions himself under the bell, clenches and unclenches his hands, then slowly starts to rise. His cheeks are red, and his legs shake with effort. It's clear that he's struggling, but he does it and rings the bell. I look down at the floor as I half-heartedly join the class in celebrating him with two claps.

It should be me up there. *Me* earning orange.

When class is over, I'm the first to leave... except I forgot that it started raining after school so I couldn't ride my bike. Mom brought me to class and arranged for Mr. Foster to bring me home. It's too far to walk, especially in the rain, so I step under the awning and wait for Haley and Mr. Foster.

"Nice necklace," says Haley when she steps outside with her dad.

Anger flares inside me, but I don't respond. I need to stay on her good side so she doesn't say anything to her dad about Chuck. I slide into the back seat and listen to Mr. Foster talk about all the places he wants to see when we all go to New York this week. Raindrops trickle down the windshield, matching my gloomy mood.

Mom notices my necklace when I get home. "Where did you get that?" she asks.

"At karate."

"Was it some kind of award or something?" she asks.

"No, I just thought it was cool," I lie, hating the monitor even more. Couldn't they at least have made it look a little less dumb?

I go to my room and shut the door, then call Rodney to tell him what happened in class.

He answers after one ring. "Hey, I was just about to call you. I don't feel right." His voice sounds kind of dull, like he just woke up from a long nap.

"Are you getting sick?" I ask.

"No, my brain just feels all foggy, and... it's so weird, but I can't remember how to play my trumpet."

I grip my phone more tightly. "What do you mean?"

"I can't remember how to hold a trumpet, which buttons to press down for each note, or how to form my lips on the mouthpiece. And when I look at music notes, I don't understand what any of them mean."

No. No, no, no. *Please, God, no.* I start to pace. "Do you remember what happened at lunch today?"

"At lunch? Um." He pauses, then says, "Not really."

"Do you remember what we did this past weekend?"

"I... I think we hung out. Maybe?" His voice is a bit panicked now. "Something's not right, Noah."

It's happened. He's been suppressed, but it got screwed up. They took more than his Gravitas memories. They took his music too.

"Rodney, I'm so sorry."

"It's not *your* fault."

Yes, it is. A lump rises in my throat. If I hadn't told him about Gravitas, Rodney would be fine right now.

But how did they know? It had to be Haley. My mind flashes back to the day I told Rodney about my powers. She could tell we were acting weird. Maybe she was even listening outside my window. And after lunch today, Rodney must have said something to confirm her suspicions.

"I've gotta go," I tell Rodney. "But I'll talk to you soon."

I immediately want to call Haley, but I hesitate.

What if I'm wrong and I just rat on myself? I put down my phone, my head swimming with what-ifs. Until I know what Haley knows—or what she *thinks* she knows—it's safer to keep my mouth shut.

Thunder rumbles outside, and lightning glints off the glass of my framed *New York Times* article. Looking at it reminds me of what Wolfshaw told me: Uncle Saul helped develop suppression.

When I see him in New York, I'll ask if he can help get Rodney's memories back.

"Noah! Slow down," calls Dad. I tap my foot and wait for my parents, eager to get a head start on the Fosters. Our flight was booked by the time they decided to go on this trip, so they won't arrive in New York for a few more hours. It's possible Uncle Saul could make contact before then.

Cold air blasts us as we walk out of the terminal, and goosebumps rise up on my arms. Grandmother is waiting for us, wearing heels and a leather jacket. If there was a *Grandmother Vogue*, she'd be on the cover.

"Noah!" She gives me a big hug, and the smell of her expensive perfume tickles my nose. "How's my favorite grandchild?" she croons.

"I'm your only grandchild!" It's our old, familiar joke.

Grandmother's car is waiting at the curb. The driver comes out to help us load our luggage in the trunk. Grandmother claims that she doesn't flaunt her wealth, even though she has a driver, lives in a fancy condo on the west side of Central Park, and wears designer clothes. She just enjoys it.

As we drive into the city from the airport, I look out the back window a few times, wondering if I'm being tailed by a Gravitas agent. Or maybe my uncle. But all I see is a lot of traffic—everyone coming to town for the Macy's Thanksgiving Day Parade. We have to drive even slower once we're in the city. When we get close to the park, the streets are closed off, and the four of us get out and walk.

It's hard to push our way through the crowds headed toward the place where the parade balloons are inflated.

"This is where the real New Yorkers are," declares Grandmother. She loves playing the tour guide, even though we've done this every year since I can remember. There's a long line of people waiting their turn to see the balloons, but Grandmother walks right to the front and we follow. After she exchanges a few words with the attendant, he slips us in, no questions asked. I always feel a little bad about cutting in line, but I'm mostly grateful that we don't have to wait for hours.

The already-inflated balloons hover over artificial turf and plastic tarps, trapped by nets so they don't float away. Long hoses stretch up and down the sidewalk and grass like veins, connecting the balloons to the machines that fill them with helium. Fans whine like giant blow-dryers, and air hisses like a hundred snakes. There's the caterpillar with its giant, colorful ball-body. And Hello Kitty. And there's a Smurf. The sun has set, and bright lights cast strangely shaped shadows over the sidewalks and the crowd.

People press in from every side, and I get separated from Mom, Dad, and Grandmother. I can still see them up ahead, but, worst-case scenario, we'll all spit out a few blocks north and reconnect.

I try to keep my eyes open for a head of wild white hair. This would be the perfect time for Uncle Saul to make an appearance.

The crews taking care of the balloons look like

they're on a hazmat team in their one-piece jumpsuits. One of them starts walking beside me.

"Which ones are your favorites?" he asks, pointing to the balloons. There's so much noise around us that I can hardly hear him.

"The superheroes." Doesn't matter if they have a cape or a web or a power sword; they're even cooler when they're supersized.

"Me too!" He puts a hand on my arm, stopping me mid-stride, and leans closer. "You would have already known that if I hadn't had to live the last ten years in hiding."

I turn to look at him. A brown beanie covers his head, and a white beard hangs down the front of his chest.

"Hello again," he says.

I was an idiot to be looking for wild white hair this whole time. I smile at my great-uncle Saul and say, "I got my pull."

"Here, put this in," Uncle Saul says, handing me a tiny earbud.

I press it into my ear, looking around to make sure nobody is paying any attention to us. Thankfully, everyone's eyes are on the balloons. We begin to walk side by side, engulfed in the crowd.

"It's good to see you again, Noah." His voice comes through clearly into my ear. "Like I said, there's so much you don't know about me. Gravitas stole that from us. Instead of being your fun uncle, I'm your Most Wanted uncle."

"Yeah, I'm sorry about that. Um... I need your help."

"Anything for my favorite nephew."

I'm too stressed to joke about me being his only nephew. "My best friend found out about Gravitas, and they suppressed him. But they screwed up and took more than just his Gravitas memories. He can't play his trumpet anymore or read music. And he was *really* good."

Uncle Saul shakes his head. "That's terrible."

"Can you help him?" I ask, turning to face Uncle Saul. The crowd parts around us.

"I'm not sure." He takes my arm and matches the plodding pace of those around us again. "Reversing suppression isn't hard. You just tell the person what they've forgotten. But if the person loses the memory of how to *do* something, especially something that took them years to learn, it may take years to remember how to do it again."

"*Years?*" I never should have told Rodney about Gravitas.

"Maybe it won't take that long for Rodney. If Gravitas botched the suppression, perhaps they didn't fully remove Rodney's ability to play. He just needs a trigger. But I can't believe they were so sloppy! Gravitas puts their mission before anything else—even people." Uncle Saul nods at my necklace. "I see that they're monitoring you. What happened?"

I give the chain a tug. "I could have earned my yellow and orange belts in one day—"

"Excellent!" he interrupts.

"Yeah, but all Gravitas cared about was the fact that

I broke the rules and practiced outside of class. They didn't even let me test for yellow."

Uncle Saul shakes his head. "Ridiculous. But don't be discouraged, Noah. Something exciting is coming for you soon. Aren't you curious about the event I mentioned?"

"Yeah!" Sure, I'm bummed about Rodney, but I've been waiting a long time to hear about this mysterious event, and we don't have much time. I'll worry about Rodney later.

We slowly shuffle by the Snoopy balloon, letting others push past us. Mom turns around and waves when she sees me, then keeps walking.

"What you don't know, and what Gravitas has never realized, is that I dropped you on a

very special night, when the moon was full and especially close to the earth. Supermoons happen a few times a year, but on the night I dropped you, there was a *super* supermoon. It was even closer than normal. These are much more rare—sometimes with intervals of five or more years between occurrences."

"Sounds cool. But why does that matter?" I ask.

"On a supermoon night, the tides rise exceptionally high, pulled by the strong gravity of the moon. I speculated that the powers of a legacy baby like you might rise as well, making you even stronger. An infant gravitar's powers are malleable and uniquely easy to manipulate, but there had to be a catalyst for it to work. When I paired the super supermoon with a surge of adrenaline by dropping you, it enhanced your powers, just as I'd hoped."

"So that's why I yanked so hard at that basketball game?"

"That's right." He smiles at me like a proud dad. "And a week from Saturday, there's going to be another super supermoon. You should start feeling it the moment the moon is out, and you'll hit your pinnacle of power at the moment the sun, earth, and moon are in perfect alignment."

"Kind of like an eclipse?" I ask.

"Kind of. They both depend on perfect alignment at

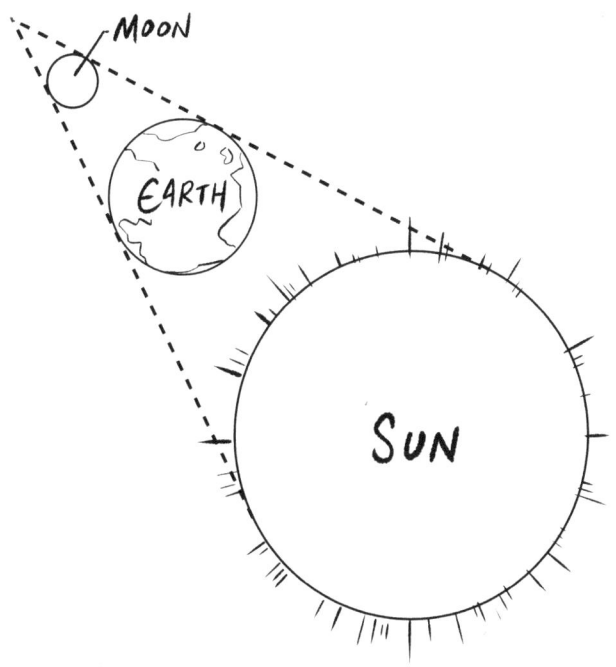

their peak. Except an eclipse happens when the moon is fully hidden in the earth's shadow, and with a supermoon, it's fully illuminated. What matters is that, now that you've got your pull, you'll be extremely powerful that night. Powerful enough to fly!"

"Really? But Gravitas says—"

"I don't care what Gravitas says. They don't understand you like I do. You'll be able to pull on the *moon* that night."

I remember Phillip's test—how he had to push himself off the floor to elevate. Even Haley can't do that yet. But if my uncle is right, I won't have to wait until I learn how to push. When Gravitas sees what I can do, I'll finally earn their respect. I'll truly be The Minor Miracle. I look up at a Buzz Lightyear balloon, soaring to infinity and beyond, and feel a surge of joy and anticipation.

Uncle Saul clears his throat. "I presume you've heard about the capsule I stole."

"I have," I say cautiously. *Mr. Foster was right. He's going to ask me to help him open the capsule.* Disappointment pokes a hole in me, and excitement drains like a slow leak.

"The gravitars on the list inside will now be grown up. There must be a few who will be expecting babies in the next year, and they deserve to know what their babies are capable of." He's getting excited, his voice loud in my ear.

"So you've been waiting all these years, hiding out, just so you can help babies eventually become super gravitars?" He may not be the monster Gravitas says he is, but I'm beginning to think that maybe my uncle *is* crazy.

Uncle Saul shakes his head. "No, I've waited all these years to confirm that my theory is correct. Now that I know it is, I want to do something about it."

"Like what? What will you do once you get that list?"

He waves his hand like he's brushing away a pesky fly. "We don't have time to flesh out all my plans."

I look ahead and realize he's right. There are only a few more balloons before we hit the end of the line.

"What's important for you to understand right now is that you can trust me. Gravitas is timid and lacks vision, so of course I make them nervous. I tried to tell them about the potential to train gravitars at a younger age, but they weren't interested. They said they wait until age twelve for a reason—end of conversation."

"It's not fair." Gravitas says rules are important, but they trained Haley earlier than twelve. Why did she get such special treatment and not me? Oh yeah. They wanted her to babysit me.

"You're right. It's *not* fair," says Uncle Saul. "It's why I tested my theory on you. You were the one legacy I had access to from birth."

"So why don't we show Gravitas that you're right? I'm your proof to get you back in!"

"Do you think the people who pushed me into hiding, who are punishing you for being extraordinary, are going to change their minds? If we go to them, they are more likely to suppress both of us."

I fiddle with the pendant on my chest and realize he's probably right.

"You could help me open that capsule next Saturday," Uncle Saul continues. "You'll have far more than twice your regular powers—plenty to match the pull of two gravitars. You'll just need to control it."

"Oh, I can control it. You should see what I can do."

"I can't wait," he says.

"But what about the other gravitar? Who's going to pull with you?"

"I was hoping you could help me find someone, Noah."

My gut churns. It's one thing to say that I'll help my uncle, but to convince someone else? The only gravitar I know well enough to ask would be Haley. No way could we convince Ms. Rule Follower to help open that capsule. I shake my head. "I don't know if I could do that. Gravitas has convinced everyone you're evil."

Uncle Saul smiles pleasantly and strokes his beard. "But now *you* know that all I want is to help legacy gravitars reach their full potential."

I look him in his light blue eyes—eyes just like mine. "Yes... but how do I get someone else to know that too?"

"You don't. Just convince them to meet you somewhere next Saturday night. Let's say the playground near your house, around midnight. Once I tell them about the supermoon and they see what you can do because of it—that you can *fly*—surely they'll be as reasonable as you are."

The crowd is dispersing up ahead. Just a couple more balloons to pass.

"It's okay if you aren't ready. Take your time. Think

about it. We can wait until the next super supermoon. I've been patient this long. I'm willing to wait until you're ready, even if it takes years."

"Really?" All I've felt since I joined Gravitas has been pressure. I like that he's not rushing me, not adding more.

"Of course. But even if you're not ready, will you please come to the playground next Saturday? So I can watch you soar through the air? It's been a dream of mine for all these years." He smiles and puts a hand on my arm. We're at the last balloon now, and the crowd is thinning. "And tomorrow, keep your eye on the balloons. Your fun uncle has something planned." Then he takes out his earbud and I hand him mine.

"Noah! We got some hot dogs," Mom calls, flagging me down.

I look behind me, wondering how I'll explain... but Uncle Saul is gone.

20

Grandmother's condo is big by Manhattan standards, and it's prime real estate since it overlooks Central Park. While Mom and Grandmother polish silver for tomorrow's Thanksgiving meal and Dad flips through channels on the TV, I wrap a large blanket around my shoulders and go out on the balcony.

I think about everything my uncle said. I'm going to have super superpowers next Saturday. I'm going to be able to do what only the most advanced gravitars can do: elevate outside. In other words, *fly*!

I look up at the half moon, then down at the people still milling about. There are guards stationed around the balloons, and parade organizers dash down sidewalks for last-minute emergencies. This must be how it looked the night I fell: everyone down below so busy that they didn't think to look up, except for that reporter. How had Uncle Saul felt, holding me, arms outstretched over the railing? Was he afraid? What if his plan hadn't worked?

A family of four crosses the street, pulling suitcases behind them, and I'm distracted from my thoughts.

"Mom, the Fosters are here!"

That night, Haley and I sleep in the living room—her on the couch, me on the floor. The condo is quiet.

"Did you see anyone or anything suspicious this afternoon?" Haley whispers.

"No." I'm more suspicious of Gravitas than I am of Uncle Saul, after talking to him today. And I'm not really in the mood to talk to Haley unless she wants to discuss why she told her dad about Rodney and got him suppressed. I bet she doesn't know that it got botched or she'd say something, but I'm not going to bring it up. Let her see for herself next week when everyone is back from break.

"Saul will probably look different than the pictures."

"No, Haley, nobody was following me. Maybe he isn't even looking for me, and Gravitas is just being paranoid."

Haley rolls over on the couch, and the city lights reflect in her eyes. "Gravitas isn't paranoid. Saul didn't drop you over the balcony for no reason. He has a plan."

"Maybe we don't know everything."

"What do you mean?" asks Haley, as if she can't imagine not knowing everything.

I roll over so I can't see her eyes. "Forget it. You're right." I make my breath slow and even so she'll think I've fallen asleep, and then I finally do.

The next morning, we settle in on the balcony, watching the parade go by and eating Grandmother's fresh-baked cinnamon rolls—fresh-baked at her favorite bakery and hand-delivered early that morning. Thick crowds have gathered along the street, cheering as each band or balloon starts off, heading down Central Park West toward Sixth Avenue.

"We're higher than the balloons! The view from up here is amazing!" says Haley.

"Best seats in the city," says Grandmother, blowing on her coffee. "It's a shame you couldn't be with us last night in the park. We'll go explore a little after the parade when the crowds die down. The stores on Fifth Avenue are decorated for Christmas."

"Hey, it's Wolf Boy—my favorite!" yells Brady.

"Who's Wolf Boy?" I ask, turning to see a balloon shaped like a creature with a wolf's body but a boy's head. Wolf Boy is looking up, mouth open, howling at a giant inflated full moon.

"It's a character from a new show where kids transform into animals," says Haley.

The balloon moves toward us, the full moon at our eye level.

Suddenly, someone down below screams. They're soon joined by others.

"What's going on?" Haley says.

"I don't know."

Something is happening down there, but the balloon blocks our view.

Wolf Boy begins to look bigger. Closer.

"It's loose!" I yell.

The giant balloon rises slowly. We're mesmerized, all of us frozen, as the larger-than-life Wolf Boy, howling at the bigger-than-life full moon, floats up past our balcony.

I have a pretty good idea who set the balloon free, and it wasn't because Wolf Boy is from his favorite show. Uncle Saul chose that balloon because of the moon, so round and full and supersized.

Before long, the balloon is above our building. I lean over Grandmother's balcony and look up. Gravitas would never have done something like that. No public displays. No fun. Mr. Foster is texting on his phone as he scans the crowd and cranes his neck to look up toward the roof of Grandmother's building. I bet he's looking for my uncle and probably texting agents on the ground. I hope Uncle Saul gets away okay.

Haley and I stay on the balcony as the adults follow

Grandmother inside and Brady uses a pair of binoculars to keep an eye on the escaped wolf balloon. He shouts out reports every few seconds and eventually runs inside to tell the adults that an ambulance has pulled up.

"Please tell me it wasn't you who pulled that balloon free," Haley whispers.

"It wasn't," I insist, slightly offended. I watch the scene below, hoping nobody was hurt.

"I didn't think so."

Then why did you ask? I want to ask, but I keep it to myself. We watch Wolf Boy as a breeze pushes him across Central Park while he continues to rise.

"Do you think they'll catch him?" Haley asks softly.

I don't know if she's talking about Uncle Saul or the balloon.

"I don't know." It's a safe answer, either way, and it's true.

"I've got posters of Dizzy Gillespie all over my room," says Rodney, flopped on my bed on Saturday afternoon.

He's here to spend the night, and I'm determined to try to help him learn to play the trumpet again. Uncle Saul said it could take years, but he also said maybe a trigger could help Rodney get his music memories back.

"It's obvious that Dizzy was my idol. I even have glasses like his! But when I play, I'm as bad as a little kid in beginning band."

It makes me boiling mad that Gravitas botched Rodney's suppression. Uncle Saul is right—Rodney was just a liability to them, and they were careless.

"Let me see your phone." Rodney passes it to me, and I search for the tuning app. The sound of one long note fills my room. I watch his face, but he stares back at me with blank eyes. "Do you know what that is?" I ask, hoping it's the trigger that will help.

"A note."

"Yeah, but what note?"

He shrugs.

"It's a D!"

"How do you know that, Noah? You aren't in band."

"You told me about it. Get out your mouthpiece and I'll show you how."

Rodney sighs, but he flips open his case. This might be the first time I've ever seen Rodney's mouthpiece resting like a silver acorn cup in the velvet, instead of shoved in his pocket. It sits beside his newly repaired trumpet.

I show him what he showed me only a week ago—how to breathe and shape his lips to find the pitch.

"Close your eyes and listen. Imagine this note is like a line that you can hang on to if you just match it."

He listens, and then he tries to match the pitch. It takes a few minutes, his D wavering between sharp and flat, but then he does it. When he connects to the note, he looks up at me with his eyebrows raised, excited.

"Hey, that felt good!" he says. He plays it again and again, until Mom knocks on the door.

"Mind helping me decorate the tree?" she asks once Rodney stops playing.

"Sure, Mrs. Minor. I'm ready for a break." Rodney puts his mouthpiece back in his case and rubs the round dent on his lips. I wonder if it feels familiar to him. It sure looks familiar to me. I've missed it.

We help Mom hang ornaments, but I'm still a bit distracted, and one slips out of my hand and shatters. I jump as Mom screams.

"Noah, that was from Grandmother!" Mom moans. "It was super expensive!"

"I'm sorry!" My heart is still racing as I head to get the broom and dustpan.

"Hey, Noah, how come you don't have The Cling?" Rodney asks as we clean up the mess. "That definitely should have made it happen."

His question catches me off guard. "Um, I guess I grew out of it. Maybe puberty," I joke. I'm amazed that it's taken this long for someone to notice.

"Remember that time you got The Cling so bad it lasted like all night?" asks Rodney.

"Yeah, that was terrible." We watched a scary movie. My pajamas didn't release until the next morning.

I wonder if there was a supermoon that night. Uncle Saul said there's a few every year and my powers would respond to them. I wasn't aligned then, so maybe my powers were all amped up and my body could only super-suck my clothes like a vacuum cleaner.

This time, my body will know exactly how to use that power. I'll be ready. I still haven't decided if I'll help my uncle or not, but I've got a little more time to choose.

★★★

"Hey, guys," Haley says, stopping by our table the next day at lunch. "What's up?"

Bold. She gets Rodney suppressed and acts like nothing happened. "Rodney's not doing great," I say.

"Yeah. I'm not sick, but my brain feels all fuzzy, and I can't remember how to play my trumpet anymore."

"*What?*" asks Haley.

"That's really weird, isn't it?" I stare at Haley intently.

She looks from me to Rodney, then back to me. "Can I talk to you, Noah? Alone?" she pleads, her voice urgent.

"Sure." I'm eager to finally have this talk with Haley now that she realizes the consequences of her actions.

"Ooh," says Rodney. A familiar look flickers in his eyes as he smiles at us. I wish Gravitas had suppressed his memories of how he teases us about being a couple.

I guide Haley to the band hall. It's empty, like I

hoped it'd be, and she follows me as I storm down the row of soundproofed practice rooms and push into the last one.

"What's going *on*?" she asks as soon as the door shuts behind us. "Did Rodney get suppressed?"

"You can stop pretending, Haley. I know you were the one who told Gravitas!"

"What are you talking about? Told them what?"

I sit down in one of the two chairs in the room, suddenly exhausted by my own fury. "I know you were suspicious about Rodney. Don't try to deny it. You had to be the one who tipped off Gravitas."

Haley doesn't sit. She stands with her hands on her hips and eyes narrowed like she's looking into my soul. "Suspicious about what, Noah?"

"That Rodney knew about Gravitas."

Her mouth hangs open for a second. "I didn't know Rodney knew about Gravitas. I swear!"

I stare at her intently, looking for signs that she's lying. Haley can be many things—like prideful and annoying—but she isn't a liar.

"How did he find out about Gravitas?" she asks.

I glance at the wall instead of meeting her piercing gaze. She knows me as well as I know her. Maybe better. She'll know if I'm lying, so I might as well tell the truth. "Okay, okay, I told him. But—"

"You *told* him?" she whisper-shrieks.

The bell rings, but neither of us move. I hate the disappointment in Haley's eyes.

"I can't believe you did that!"

Neither can I. "I know, I know. I didn't mean to, okay? But I had to. Chuck had Rodney's trumpet, and he was going to throw it in the trash. I had to stop him. I didn't know Rodney was watching when I pulled Chuck down the hall."

Haley goes into full-blown Mom Mode. "You can't use your powers whenever you feel like it, Noah, like some sort of vigilante. You aren't being trained to be a middle school superhero. You're training to be a secret agent, and that means you follow Gravitas rules."

"I *know*." I feel like I'm being repeatedly run over by a truck.

"Wait . . . how did Gravitas know about Rodney?" asks Haley. She stares at the wall, completely in her own head. "And why didn't Gravitas suppress *you* too?"

"*Excuse* me?" I say. "That's pretty harsh."

"If they knew you told Rodney, they would have suppressed you too," insists Haley.

She has a point.

"Maybe because they still need me to catch Uncle Saul?" I suggest.

Haley gasps, like something has just horrified her. "What if Rodney wasn't suppressed by Gravitas?"

I shake my head. "How is that even possible? They're the only ones who even know what suppression means."

Haley raises her eyebrows. "Saul helped develop the suppression program."

I fight the uneasy feeling that creeps into my gut.

"Don't you think it's weird that he hasn't made contact yet?" asks Haley. "Maybe he has and you don't even realize it. Maybe he has you bugged or something."

She doesn't know about the three times he *has* been in contact, but I'm not going to confess to that right now. Not when she's already mad at me.

"But even if he did, why would Uncle Saul suppress Rodney?" I ask instead, evading her question. I remind myself that all my uncle wants to do is help gravitar babies reach their full potential, like he helped me.

She gets up and begins to pace as she follows this new theory. "I don't know why he'd do it, but I bet he *could*. We just need to figure out Saul's motive."

"Hang on, hang on." I hold up my hands. "Don't be so quick to—"

"He'd know that Gravitas wants you to turn him in. So maybe he doesn't want you to trust Gravitas. Since he hasn't made contact, of course you'd assume that Gravitas suppressed Rodney! You'd be mad at them, so when he *does* make contact, you'd already be on his side."

I don't want to believe that I could be so easily fooled, but now I go over my conversations with Uncle Saul through a new lens—especially the last one. He seemed so sympathetic to my problem. I thought I was keeping this important secret with him—that we really could change the world for the better. But what if, all this time, he was tricking me? It's clear that Gravitas wasn't involved in Rodney's suppression or I'd be suppressed too. I know in my gut Haley is right about that.

I look up at her. She has stopped pacing and is studying me.

"Noah." There's so much disappointment in the way she says my name. "Saul made contact with you, didn't he? When? In New York?"

I take a deep breath and do the hardest thing I've ever done. I tell Haley the truth about both times I've seen my uncle and tell her his plan for Saturday night. Haley stays calm, listening carefully and asking questions—showing all the control and clarity needed to be a good agent.

"Okay, what if he put a bug in your room when he came the first time?" she asks.

"He left that snow globe for me, but Gravitas tested it. It was clean."

"Yeah, but what about the rest of your room?"

Why didn't I think about that? If Uncle Saul bugged my room, he heard all my conversations with Rodney and he'd know how to frame Gravitas—and fool me.

"I am such a feckless dolt."

22

Haley and I search my room for the bug, using the device her dad used to test my snow globe. It has a range of about a foot, so we have to be close for it to detect anything. We move slowly and quietly, even though I want to tear my room apart. If Uncle Saul is listening, he won't know we're searching for a bug or realize we're onto him. It isn't attached to the bottom of my bed or on the blades of the ceiling fan or down in the toe of a shoe.

We eventually find it behind my framed *New York Times* article. My heart sinks. If I had just told Gravitas the first time I saw him, they would have found the bug and Uncle Saul would probably be suppressed by now. Rodney would still be able to play his trumpet, and... So many consequences fall like dominoes as I play back the events of the last two months.

I motion Haley outside, safely out of bug range. "I have more bad news. I told Rodney that you're a gravitar when we were in my room. Uncle Saul knows."

"Then I should be the one who shows up with you in the park this Saturday." She doesn't sound afraid or mad. Honestly, she sounds excited.

"Do you think your dad will let you?" I ask.

She shrugs. "We'll ask. But for that to happen, you know what we need to do, right?"

I sigh. "Right. We need to tell him."

"It's the only hope you have of staying in the program when this is all over."

There's no hope of me staying in the program. I realize that, and Haley will, too, if she's honest with herself. Gravitas will use me to catch Uncle Saul, like they've been planning all along, and then suppress me. I'll lose everything after they get what they want.

"With great power there must also come—great responsibility!"

At least, that's what I keep telling myself. I just hope that, on Saturday night, The Minor Miracle gets to fly one time and I get to be the superhero I've always dreamed of being before Gravitas takes it away.

In class that afternoon, I earn my yellow belt, easily pulling the benderball across the mat. When Mr. Foster ties the belt around my waist, he also removes my

necklace monitor. "We trust you, Noah," he says, and I feel like a worm.

On the drive home, I clear my throat and do the second-hardest thing I've ever done: I tell Mr. Foster everything. Haley sits beside me in the back seat for moral support. He ends up circling the neighborhood, and aside from his knuckles turning white as he grips the steering wheel, he doesn't freak out nearly as much as I thought he would.

"I'm really sorry. This is all my fault."

"You got that right." He shoots a glance at me, his jaw clenched.

"But at least we know now. Right, Dad?" says Haley. "And Saturday night at the park, Noah and I—"

"No," says Mr. Foster, holding up a hand. "Midnight on Saturday, you will be safe at home, Haley."

"But, Dad! Saul *knows* I'm a gravitar and he hasn't come for me. Why be so overprotective?"

"He shouldn't know *anything* about you. Maybe I should assign you a bodyguard."

"No!" Haley slumps against her seat. "That's not necessary."

"It is. Definitely on Saturday, when we know Saul will be in town. I'm sorry, Haley, but there is no way I would willingly let you be in the park with that evil man. The only reason I'm okay with Noah being there is because we don't have a choice if we want to catch Saul."

Haley stares out the window, fuming, but I'm secretly relieved.

"With great power there must also come—great responsibility!"

It's my fault Haley's life is in danger, and I should be the one who is responsible for catching him, even if that puts me in danger. I could never forgive myself if something happened to her.

"Noah, we don't have much time before Saturday." Mr. Foster pulls into my driveway. "Be prepared to work hard in class on Wednesday."

On Wednesday, Mr. Foster tells the class that we're all going to start learning how to slug.

Dawson raises his hand. "I thought only orange belts practiced slugging."

What a turd burglar.

"Not today." Mr. Foster glances at me. I know he's worried that he doesn't have time to fully prepare me for whatever will happen Saturday night—worried that the boy he convinced Gravitas to train will be an utter failure. I won't let him down if I can help it.

Mr. Foster takes a bag out of the closet and hands each yellow belt a ball about the size of a benderball, but a little heavier and without any holes.

"Learning to slug means starting at the beginning again," says Mr. Foster. "*SLG* stands for 'slow-let-go' because you have to *slowly* let go of your desire line. If you don't, it could be dangerous. Drop too fast while elevated, and you could get hurt. Or killed. Orange belts, if you have mastered slugging at least half your weight, you can strap into a harness and practice letting yourself down from the ceiling."

Dawson is the only orange belt who grabs a slugging ball. The rest of the orange belts have progressed to their harnesses already, and I can tell that it irks him. This makes me happier than it should.

"Embedded in these slugging trainers are accelerometers. They measure how quickly the ball falls. Too fast, and it beeps. The faster the fall, the higher the beep." He drops the ball without slugging, and a high-pitched beep fills the room. It's so piercing that we cover our ears. "Control is key when slugging. Remember, you must *slowly* let go of your powers. This is far different than just ceasing to pull. It's careful and deliberate."

Yeah, but *how* do we slug? I'm impatient. Saturday is looming.

"Similar to getting your pull, you'll have to find your own way to your slug. It's harder than a pull because it isn't just a skill. You have to be willing to *let go* of your desire line—let go of what you want—which hurts. It burns. You must embrace the pain, hold on to it. A slug requires strength of character and determination in the face of pain."

Okay, enough talking. I'm ready. Bring it on.

"Begin by bending at waist level and pulling the ball from the mat to your chest," Mr. Foster explains. "Then slowly release your pull, slugging the ball back to the mat at a controlled, steady rate. You'll know you have it when you feel a burning sensation and the ball hits the ground without beeping. Then you can progress to heavier balls. Begin."

We all bend at the waist and get started. I pull the ball to my chest easily, but as soon as I let go, it falls to the mat fast.

BEEP!

"Imagine you're holding a heavy weight. You bend your arms to lift it to your chest. Then imagine slowly letting the weight back down until your arms are fully extended again. Resist releasing the weight too quickly."

He makes it sound so easy, but my ball drops swiftly to the floor again, triggering another shrill beep. I'm willing to *endure* the pain, but how do I even *find* the pain?

Pull, release.

BEEP!

Pull, release.

BEEP!

I look up to see that Dawson has already advanced to slugging a five-pound ball.

Slugging. It sounds like *sluggish,* lagging behind—which I'm doing again.

If I'm supposed to *feel* pain, maybe I have to *think* about pain too. Like about how Uncle Saul tricked me.

And how Rodney is the real victim.

BEEP!

It's all my fault.

BEEP!

How can I help my friend?

BEEP!

He needs more than middle C.

BEEP! BEEP! BEEP!

"Remember to let go *slowly*. Feel the burn," says Mr. Foster.

This isn't working. I'm not a weight lifter. Just like I'm not a knitter. I need to find my own way to slug, like Mr. Foster said. I bend over again and pull the ball to my chest, searching my mind for a memory that might help.

One Thanksgiving, Grandmother asked me to carry her beloved crystal pitcher to the table for breakfast. It was filled with orange juice and so heavy that I had to use two hands to hold it. I remember how I tried to set it down slowly, but the pitcher was too heavy, and I was too little. It hit the shiny wood table with a thud, sloshing OJ all over and leaving a big dent.

As I start to release my pull on the slugging trainer, I hold on to the memory of trying to set down Grandmother's crystal pitcher. I start to feel a burn in my chest... *yes!* But the moment I take my concentration off the ball, it swiftly falls.

BEEP!

"Keep practicing. In basketball, players practice free throws over and over again until they can make one without even thinking. It's called muscle memory. The same concept works for pulling and slugging."

I can tell he threw out that particular example for my benefit. But I need to *have* my slug before I can start working on the muscle memory. With a sense of urgency, I bend over, pull the ball, and try again.

As I keep trying, the two words won't leave me. *Muscle memory.* Our bodies can remember how to do something, even when we're not thinking about it.

My focus shifts from the ball, and it drops with another piercing **BEEP!**

What if muscle memory is the key to helping Rodney? Uncle Saul was wrong about a lot of things, but he could be right about the trigger. I just haven't found the right one yet, but I don't have to do it alone anymore.

Haley loves the idea of triggering Rodney's music memories, and we work on a plan for the next three days. By Saturday evening, I'm full of anticipation, imagining how Rodney's music will come flooding back to him. I'm also excited to see what happens when the moon comes out. Tonight is going to be absolutely **EPIC!**

But when I think about seeing Uncle Saul at the park, tendrils of fear creep through me. Will he know that I know he's been lying?

Mr. Foster is worried too. He insisted on having an agent assigned to Haley and me tonight. When I get to the gym, the crowd is so big that even if I knew who Mr. Foster had tailing us, it would be impossible to pick them out. We haven't had a game since before Thanksgiving, and the stands are almost full.

Haley is sitting with her mom and Brady, who's

wearing my old Superman cape, stomping on the bleachers with his cowboy boots, and making a racket. Haley gives me a thumbs-up and I give her two back. I wish I felt as confident as my thumbs.

Some of the band kids are sitting up high against the back wall with Rodney, their instruments primed and ready to play. Part of the plan Haley and I came up with was for Rodney to try to play at the game. When I asked his band friends if they'd be his backup, they were all over it.

Rodney waves his trumpet and plays the first few notes of "We Will Rock You." It's not even close to what he's capable of, but maybe playing at the game will give him the confidence to try something harder. For the first time since he lost his memories, he looks excited.

I look up and see the remnants of pink clouds through the small windows of the gym. The moon is rising out there, and I feel an itch beneath the surface of my skin. My power rises like a tide, and I suddenly feel all amped up, like I just drank three sodas in a row. I want to spin a desire line, certain I could pull myself to the moon if there was an opening in the gym. It's a lot of power—more than I've ever felt before—and I'm struck by a new set of nerves as I remember what happened the last time I lost control during a game. A lot of people could get seriously hurt with this kind of power left unchecked.

Thankfully, Coach benches me from the start. We score the first points, and Rodney and his band friends stand and play. "We will, we will rock you!" Some people in the crowd sing along, and Rodney looks like he's having fun.

Chuck isn't. He quickly commits three fouls and misses every shot he takes.

"Noah! You're in," calls Coach as he takes Chuck out. He pats me on the back with his clipboard before I trot out onto the floor.

Chuck glares at me when he comes off the court, like it's my fault he's playing badly. The last thing I need is Chuck's attitude. I'm having enough trouble worrying about controlling the power that surges through me, begging to be released.

The moon is now fully out, shining round and bright through the windows of the gym. I jump up and down on the court, unable to stand still.

Andy gets the ball downcourt but is surrounded by opposing players trying to steal it. He quickly passes to me, and I take off toward our basket. I feel like I'm running on one of those moving sidewalks at the airport, each step propelling me farther than it should. I can just barely keep up with myself. My powers course through me, fast and furious, like an out-of-control caffeine buzz.

I get to the basket and leap, arms extended, eager to

slam the ball through the net. I'm not thinking, just feeling, caught up in the moment and flying high . . . until my hand hits the metal rim.

CLANG!

I miss the shot and fall to the court. Pain blazes through my right wrist, and I cradle it as I kneel on the shiny wood under the basket.

The ref blows his whistle, and Coach runs onto the court and crouches beside me. "Noah, are you okay?"

"I hurt my wrist."

He examines it tenderly and calls a trainer to take a look once we're on the sidelines. My parents come down to check on me as the trainer wraps my wrist in a bandage and gives me an ice pack. "I'm pretty sure it's a sprain," he says.

"Well, that was one heck of a jump," says Coach. "Too bad you just put yourself out of the game."

Mom wants to leave immediately and go to a clinic, but I beg her to wait until tomorrow. If I leave, it will ruin our plan to help Rodney. Dad helps convince her, then lingers behind as she makes her way back up the stands.

"I'm proud of you for going for that shot. Your vertical was incredible."

"Thanks, Dad." I'm glad Dad is impressed, after I've been such a disappointment to Gravitas. Maybe by helping them catch Uncle Saul tonight, I'll earn their respect and avoid getting suppressed.

I spend the rest of the game on the bench, where I have a hard time paying attention. The moon is moving in line with the sun and the earth, already pulling high and dangerous tides along certain coasts. Already pulling me. I feel drawn to it, distracted from the game.

The Rim Rock Mustangs pull out a win in the final seconds. The fans in the stands explode into cheers, and the trumpets blare. I keep my right wrist close to my chest and pound my left fist in the air, yelling at the top of my lungs. It sounds like a battle cry. I'm ready to meet Uncle Saul in the park and defend all that is true, good, and beautiful.

But first, I'm going to help my friend get his music back.

As the gym clears out, Haley, Rodney, and I head to the band hall—the band director left it unlocked for us, eager to try anything to get his star musician back. Our parents agreed to let us stay late to help Rodney. His mom is supposed to pick us up in two hours and take us home.

I catch a glimpse of the shadow of our Gravitas bodyguard lurking behind as we make our way into Rodney's favorite practice room at the end of the hall.

"You ready?" I ask Rodney.

"Ready!" he says, raising his trumpet.

"Okay, listen to this." Haley holds up her phone, and a trumpet plays a slow jazz tune.

Rodney closes his eyes. "Hey," he says after a minute. "This is one of my dad's songs."

"That's right." I hope it doesn't make him mad. We watch as Rodney listens for a minute, his head cocked.

"It's one of his first hits," says Rodney, opening his eyes. "He wrote it when I was just a baby." His fingers push on the valves of his trumpet. "One of my earliest memories is of carrying around Dad's mouthpiece, blowing into it to figure out the different sounds I could make with just my lips."

"It's working!" says Haley.

I hold up a hand, stopping her words like a crossing guard so she doesn't distract Rodney. He has a long way to go if he's going to move from distant baby memories to playing the way he could before. How far can he get before midnight, when I meet Uncle Saul?

"When I got a little older, he would put his big hands on mine to help me hold the trumpet and learn fingerings," Rodney says.

The jazz tune ends and a new track begins. It's the same song, but this time, only the first few seconds loop on repeat.

"Why don't you try playing along?" I say softly. "See if you can remember."

Rodney slowly lifts his trumpet to his lips.

He takes a deep breath and closes his eyes, then plays. Haley and I remain quiet as Rodney flounders for the right notes, hitting some and missing others. Gradually, he matches a few in a row, then more, until he's able to play the short loop.

It *is* working!

I nod to Haley, and she switches to the next track. Same song, but this time playing a little more of it. We've got the whole song ready to go, broken down into sections, each one slightly longer than the last. Each time Rodney masters one loop, we move to the next, letting him work it out. It's not perfect, but it's clear that he's getting a little bit smoother with each note he plays.

Haley slips off her shoes, and we sit on the floor, leaning against the wall as we listen to Rodney. My wrist is sensitive, so I hold it still, keeping my hand high to stop it from throbbing. I'm so in the zone that I barely hear Haley when she whispers, "I've got to go to the bathroom." She stands, and Rodney stops playing.

"You sound great. Keep going. I'll be right back," she says and slips out the door, grabbing her shoes at the last minute.

"It's working!" I say. "It will take some practice to get back to where you were before, making your own music, but you're already way better than 'We Will Rock You'!"

Rodney rubs the deep indent left on his lips by his mouthpiece. He's been playing nonstop for almost an hour. "Thanks. I mean it. *Thank you.*"

"You're welcome."

"Do you mind if we keep going?" asks Rodney.

"Of course not."

He puts his trumpet to his lips just as we hear Haley scream.

24

I immediately jump up and run down the hall, Rodney close behind me.

"Noah!" Haley yells from the band director's office. Her voice is panicked, something I've never heard before. And then Uncle Saul comes out, and before I can do anything, a force pulls my feet out from under me and I land on my back.

Pain shoots through my wrist and up my arm. I try to ignore it as I'm pulled along with music stands and plastic chairs across the band hall floor, toward the office. Trophies fly off the shelf behind us and crash to bits on the floor. Shards smack my leg.

Uncle Saul retches.

That was a colossal yank, not a pull. He's not in control. I could easily use my powers to beat him.

"Noah, what's going on?" Rodney is on his back beside me, his eyes wide with fear.

I don't have time to explain. "You need to get out of here!"

Suddenly, the room goes dark as my uncle presses tape to my eyes. Then he binds my hands behind my back, and pain surges through my arm from my injured wrist as he pulls me to standing. I can feel his hot breath on my neck, and then he's gone, moved somewhere else to do who knows what.

"Uncle Saul! Why are you doing this?"

I hear scuffling.

"Don't touch me! I'm—"

Rodney doesn't finish his sentence. *What's happening?* A door slams. I need to do something, need to use my pull, but I didn't take the time to focus on anything before my eyes got covered. If I pull randomly, I'll likely miss my target and could end up knocking myself out.

"Are y'all okay? What's going on? He put tape on my eyes. I can't see anything!" Haley is being Haley, trying to be in control even now.

"He did the same to me, but I'm all right! He's got Rodney, though," I call out.

"Have a seat," my uncle whispers in my ear as he pushes down on my shoulders. My knees bend and I land in a chair. He's behind me. I can't pull him yet.

"If you try to pull me, your friends get hurt," Uncle Saul says.

"Don't listen to him, Noah! Don't help him open that capsule!" Haley continues to rant, threatening violence and demanding to be set free, but Rodney remains silent. That isn't good.

"Is Rodney okay?" I ask.

"He is. He's just very sleepy. I took care of that pesky agent too. Lucky for me, I had some heavy-duty sedatives. He'll be sleeping for hours."

"There was an agent in the *school*?" I ask, faking surprise. The tape tugs at my raised eyebrows.

"Hold on. I need to apply a little more tape to your friend Haley," says Uncle Saul. I can hear her yelling for a little while longer, and then I can't. Just an enraged "MMM! Mmmm-mmmmm-MMMM!" He must have taped her mouth shut.

I'm sure she's seething.

"I thought I could trust you, Noah, but I knew I couldn't trust Gravitas. I was worried that they were watching you. Imagine my surprise when I got to the park a little early and found it crawling with agents."

"No way! I had no idea!" I've got to play dumb, pretend I had no idea about the plan Mr. Foster put together for tonight.

"Hmm." Uncle Saul sounds unconvinced. "Either way, I decided to pivot. When I came to watch you at the game, I clocked another agent keeping tabs on you and the girl. There's only one reason Gravitas would have agents at the park and assigned to you. I can't believe you told them about our little meeting, Noah!"

"I didn't! The only person I told was Haley—and just enough so that she'd come to the park with me tonight. I promise!"

"You told that kid Rodney about me," Uncle Saul says, his voice dangerously low.

"Why would you think that?" I need him to think I'm clueless about the bug.

Uncle Saul ignores my question and just sighs.

"It's not too late for us to execute your plan. Maybe we could open the capsule here instead of at the park?"

"Exactly what I was thinking!" My uncle claps me on the back, then tightens his grip on my shoulder. "But there's only one way to know if I can trust you, Noah. Once you and Haley open the capsule, I'll need you to come with me."

"Come with you? What do you mean?"

"I'll need you to convince the gravitars on the list that my theory works. That their children will be just as powerful as you are. When they see what you can do, they won't be able to resist. And if they do . . ." He hesitates, then chuckles. "Well, sometimes we have to do unpleasant things for the greater good of humankind."

Uncle Saul's as dangerous as everyone kept telling me he was. If I help him open it, Haley and Rodney may go free, but what about all the gravitars on that list? He's not beyond kidnapping, maybe worse, to get what he wants. I have to find a way to stop him. It's my fault we're in this mess in the first place. I should have told Gravitas about Uncle Saul from the beginning. I never should have trusted him.

"I'll go with you, as long as you don't hurt Rodney or Haley."

"Your friends will be just fine as long as you don't betray me. We'll leave Rodney here, but Haley comes to the roof with us. If she's a good little girl and helps open the capsule, I'll leave her there to be rescued."

Haley hasn't stopped furiously *mmm-mmm-mmm*ing from the office. I'm not so sure that she's prepared to be a *"good little girl."*

"What if she refuses to help?"

"We'll threaten to kill Brady if she doesn't comply."

I grit my teeth and clench my hands. I'll play along until I come up with a plan. One thing I know for certain: Uncle Saul isn't laying a hand on Brady.

I feel his cool hands on my hurt wrist. "I'm not a terrible man. But Gravitas stole my family from me when they forced me into hiding. I couldn't visit my own sister, your grandmother, and I'm tired of being alone. Yes, I want to help legacy children, but I want more. You and I, we can be partners *and* family."

My mind races as Uncle Saul retrieves Haley and guides us through the halls of the school. My eyes are still taped and my hands still tied, and judging by her lack of resistance, the same is true of Haley. If there's something I could pull at him, I can't see it. And if I pull *him,* he'll just come hurtling at Haley and me. That won't work—our hands are literally tied.

Suddenly, Uncle Saul pulls us to a halt. "Haley, you're going to help us open the capsule."

"MMM-mmmMMM!"

"I would hate for something to happen to your little brother. What's his name again? Brady? Now, tell me you'll cooperate."

I hear the snick of tape pulling from skin, and Haley yells, "I won't let you touch him! You weasel!"

I hear the zip of a backpack. "You don't have much choice. Feel that, Haley?"

Haley stops her tirade abruptly, letting me know that something isn't right.

"What is it, Haley? Uncle Saul, what are you doing?"

"I have a syringe with enough sedative to put a full-grown man to sleep. But for a little thing like you, Haley... who knows what it would do? Either you help me open the capsule, or you won't be awake—maybe not even alive—to save Brady."

I move in the direction of her heavy breathing and lean into her, trying to transfer some warmth and comfort. She leans back, so hard I almost stumble.

Uncle Saul starts walking us again, then guides us into what sounds like a stairwell, echoey and cold. We walk up two flights of stairs, and Haley keeps her mouth shut. The door creaks open, and cold air blows into the narrow stairwell.

It's even colder when Uncle Saul leads us out. He rips the tape off my eyes.

"Ow!"

"Sorry. It's better to do it fast."

I glance around quickly. The first thing I see is Uncle Saul holding a syringe at Haley's neck. It makes me sick. I look away and see that we're on a wide expanse of flat roof, about half the size of a football field. The surface is rough, like someone poured black tar across it and then tossed in handfuls of gravel while it was still wet. It's empty except for a big metal box in the middle of the space. Rusted and ancient, it's about the size and shape of a refrigerator lying on its side. It's the only thing that I could potentially pull, but it's so big that it's more likely to crush us all instead of just immobilizing Uncle Saul.

"When the capsule opens, the GPS will activate and alert Gravitas. We'll have to make a fast getaway," he says. "Turn around; I'll cut your hands free so you can run when it's time."

I feel a glimmer of hope, glancing over my shoulder to catch Uncle Saul off guard the moment he takes the needle from Haley's neck to set me free. I'll pull him hard, make him stumble and fall. Maybe he'll accidentally inject himself. But instead, he uses his free hand to pull a pair of scissors from his back pocket. The needle never drops from its position against Haley's neck, even when he cuts the rope from around my hands.

Haley remains blind and restrained. She shivers in her thin Rim Rock Mustangs T-shirt, her feet still bare. Haley—always so strong, spunky, in charge—looks so vulnerable. Even scared. I want to scoop her up and carry her far away from here.

Uncle Saul guides us to the box, the tip of the deadly needle still at Haley's neck. He readjusts it as he pulls the capsule awkwardly out of his backpack. I consider trying to pull him again, but Haley and the syringe

would likely come with him, and she could still get stuck with the needle. I have to bide my time and wait for the perfect moment.

Uncle Saul sets the capsule reverently in the middle of the box. It looks like it's sitting on a sacrificial altar.

"Haley will pull from over there with me." He points to the other side of the box. "You stay on this side." I can't see Haley's eyes, but she seems resigned, silent and defeated. Uncle Saul quickly undoes the ties on her hands behind her back and restrains them at the front, then guides her into position.

If I knew how to push, I'd send Uncle Saul right over the edge of the roof.

"Kneel down, both of you." He uses one of his legs to hit Haley behind her knees, and she buckles to the ground.

"Ow!" she cries.

"Hey! You promised not to hurt her!"

"She's fine." He pulls some string from his backpack and uses the tape he pulled off my eyes to attach it to the capsule's lid. He hands the other end of the string to Haley. "Now you know where to pull. The end of this line is the capsule."

I guess he doesn't trust her enough to untape her eyes.

"Let's do this!" Uncle Saul looks so pumped. "I've waited twelve years for this night, Noah, to see your powers full-blown."

I wish I could figure out how to use my full-blown powers to pull Haley to safety, but the box is in the way, and there is no safe place up on this roof anyway.

"The tricky part will be pulling evenly." Uncle Saul ducks down so I can just see his head above the edge of the box.

"Right." I consider pulling the capsule early and keeping the lives of who knows how many people safe... but I can't. He'd hurt Haley.

"I trust you, Noah." Uncle Saul fixes me with an intense gaze. "You are my legacy. Our future. Just look at that moon."

I look up and see it—round and full and somehow heavy, hanging in the sky, calling to me. I stand without realizing it, my eyes fixed on the bright globe. Something deep inside me wants the moon. Wants to rise up to it.

"Kneel back down," says Uncle Saul. "Settle. Later, you can fly. But you don't need all that power for the capsule. Just the strength of two gravitars."

I shift my gaze back to the silver capsule and kneel again, praying all goes well. Like, really praying.

God, please help.

"Ready?" Uncle Saul asks.

"Ready."

Uncle Saul counts down, "Three, two, one, pull!"

The gravitons spin into a thread faster than I've ever spun before. The pull is almost immediate, the power something I've never felt. I'm reeling in something big and splashy—a marlin or a shark.

The capsule flies at me so fast that I have to duck. The momentum sends it skittering across the roof, and it stops just short of the edge.

I look at my uncle and see him standing, the needle at Haley's neck.

"What happened?" she asks.

"I pulled too hard."

"Yes, you did. Get the capsule, Noah." Uncle Saul's voice is quiet. "And pull gradually next time, matching our strength."

Haley is visibly trembling, her body hunched with her shoulders up around her ears. I wish I could see her

eyes. It's hard to know if she's terrified or just cold.

I pull on the capsule, and it comes clattering across the roof. It stings when it hits my hand. I set it back on the metal box.

"Let's try this again." He puts the needle away and hands the string back to Haley so she knows where to direct her desire line.

The bitter wind makes my face numb. "I'm ready."

"All right. Three, two, one, pull!"

Again, we pull. Gravitons bind into a thick, strong rope, and I feel the force gathering in me, but I breathe deeply and will myself to slow down. To pull lightly. To match the pull from the other side of the capsule, like matching a pitch on Rodney's trumpet.

"Go easy," Uncle Saul yells at me.

"I'm trying." My teeth clench with the effort to restrain myself.

"Pull *harder*, Haley," my uncle commands.

The capsule inches toward me, then toward Uncle Saul and Haley; it stabilizes, then moves toward me again, forcing the other two to pull harder. I spend more effort trying to curb my power than using it. The capsule trembles. I focus on it, squinting my eyes so it is all I can see.

POP!

I stop pulling as soon as the lid comes off, and the capsule hurtles at Haley, who must not have stopped pulling.

SMACK!

She goes limp and slumps to her side, all but her head hidden by the box, as the capsule rolls back onto the metal.

"Haley!" I yell.

My eyes lock with my uncle's and then dart back to the capsule. I pull at the same time as he does, and the capsule hangs suspended between us. But he can't beat me. I'm more powerful than he is—supermoon powerful—and he knows it.

So he lets go. Suddenly, the capsule hurtles toward me like it's been shot out of a slingshot. I dodge, and it clatters on the roof behind me. I turn and see it roll to a stop, then look over my shoulder to check what my uncle's next move will be.

He's on the other side of the roof, at the edge, holding Haley in his arms. Her head flops and her legs dangle—she's still unconscious.

"I thought I could trust you!" Uncle Saul yells. "Traitor!"

His eyes are wild and manic. If he drops her—

"No!" I run toward them, even though I know I can't get to them fast enough to stop Uncle Saul. I have no plan; I'm just pushed by the adrenaline that surges through my body as the sun, earth, and moon align and my powers peak.

I watch in horror as my uncle drops her. But I don't stop running.

Time seems to slow down. Haley fills my thoughts and my heart. There's no room for myself in there. I have to save her.

Maybe he's using Haley like bait, to get me away from the capsule. Don't care. If I get out of Uncle Saul's line of sight, he can't pull me, so I leap over the edge, shooting a desire line to Haley. I pull her as hard as I can to slow her descent, even as I begin to fall. I haven't learned how to spin more than one desire line at a time. The strength of my pull stops her fall, but the momentum sends Haley flying above me like a rag doll.

I turn my focus up, up, up, past Haley, to the moon, doing what Gravitas says is impossible. I'm just feet from the ground when my desire line catches, and I begin rising fast—toward Haley, who is beginning to fall again. Her wrists are still tied together, which

means that as she falls, her arms form a circle, like she's making a basketball hoop for me to shoot through.

That's exactly what I do, diving up through her arms so they encircle my neck. My wrist screams in pain as I tightly grip her waist, ensuring she won't fall as we both rise on my desire line hooked to the moon. When we get level with the roof of the school, I see Uncle Saul holding the capsule and gawking at us. He could pull us both—get us back on the roof.

I give a strong tug, zooming Haley and me upward with lightning speed. We keep rising, even when I let go of my line and spin another to pull the capsule out of my uncle's hands. I feel resistance as he tries to pull it back, but he's no match for my supermoon powers. The capsule flies out into the air, toward Haley and me.

"Nooooo!" Uncle Saul's frustrated wail echoes through the night.

I release the silver capsule and respin my desire line to the moon, following the trajectory of the capsule as it tumbles to the ground. I'm expecting to have to switch desire lines again, to keep playing this game of cat and mouse so that Uncle Saul can't get either Haley or the capsule, but he runs back into the school. *He's giving up already?* Then I hear the sound of cars screeching into the parking lot. Gravitas is here.

Power courses through me like electricity. Buoyed

by my victory and the call of the moon, I rise fast. We go up and up... and I realize that I don't know how to get us back down. If I let go, we'll fall. I can't slug a tiny ball; there's no way I can slug Haley and me.

"Haley, wake up!" She jerks awake and squirms in my arms. "Steady! Be careful."

I let go of her waist briefly and rip the tape off her eyes. We're so high that we can see the lights of downtown glittering in the distance.

"Where's Saul? What's going on?" She sounds scared. She should be.

"He dropped you. I jumped." I look back at the moon. The air is starting to get colder. I can't feel the tips of my fingers.

"You did what?"

"I *jumped*. To save you."

Haley looks down and then wraps her legs around me like a baby monkey. "Noah, how are you doing this? Are you pushing off the ground from way up here?"

"No, I'm pulling on the moon!"

"That's impossible."

"Really, Haley?" I'd like to relish the fact that I can finally do something that Haley can't, but it's hard, because we're going to die.

"Well, however you're doing it, you've got to get us down!" Haley says. "Slug!"

"Can't." I think about my last gravitar class—the loud

beeps as the ball kept hitting the ground. "I haven't learned to slug! You do it."

"Noah." Her voice is calm but strained. "I can't slug on your line. *You* have to do it." She's shivering again, this time clearly from the increasingly cold air. I try to hold her tighter and share warmth.

My ears start to pop, like we're in an airplane.

"Noah... you've got to... let go," she says.

She sounds like she's having a hard time thinking. And breathing. So am I.

Can't... keep... rising. Have... to try...

I let go of my pull, but we drop too quickly. Haley screams and I panic, wildly spinning a new desire line as we tumble. I hook the moon and pull hard on the line. We jerk up so fast that my grip on Haley slips.

"Slowly!" Haley warns as I regain my hold on her. "You can do it, Noah!" Her cheek presses against mine.

We're still rising. And it's getting harder and harder to concentrate as fear clouds my mind.

We're going to get hit by a plane. Run out of oxygen. Freeze to death.

"Noah, y-y-you've already d-d-done the hardest part!" says Haley through chattering teeth.

"W-w-what?" I feel like Haley and I are turning into an ice sculpture.

"Y-y-you risked it all. Y-y-you let go and j-j-jumped."

"Let go slowly. Feel the burn," Mr. Foster's calm voice repeats in my head.

He said we need to find our own way, and I need to find mine now. I slip into a zone, thinking about all I was willing to give up to save Haley's life.

I told Uncle Saul I'd go with him, give up my very life, to save her.

"Let go slowly. Feel the burn."

I jumped, knowing I could die, to save her.

"Let go slowly. Feel the burn."

My chest feels like a rope is running through it—the burn. I've got it, but is it strong enough to slug us both? I keep my eyes closed, focusing on all the big and little things I was willing to lose in this world when I jumped, unbraiding my life to save my friend.

I was willing to give up Rodney... my parents... my comic... the robot slide...

"Good, Noah. You're doing it," Haley whispers.

The burn hurts less as I remember the things I love. I would have jumped for Rodney, jumped for my parents, for the Fosters. I would give up turkey cookies and trumpet farts and all the things in life that make it sweet.

"Noah, when you're ready, open your eyes," says Haley softly.

I'm ready.

I open my eyes and see that we're almost to the ground.

We touch down lightly. Back to earth. Back to ordinary, dirt-on-the-ground earth. It feels entirely different from the day I got my pull, dragging a turkey-shaped cookie across my bedroom floor. I am not filled with confidence and joy that bursts from my chest like I've won Olympic gold. I am filled with peace and determination, glowing warm and quiet like embers after a fire, as I release my desire line.

I did it. I endured the pain—the risk of losing it all—and it was worth it.

"Thanks for saving my life, Noah," Haley says. I look into her eyes, and I swear that if there was a speech bubble over my head, it would say, **MY HERO!** I may have saved Haley's life, but she went and saved me right back.

I realize I've still got my arms around her waist, and I let go, but she doesn't. She kisses me on the cheek. Just a peck. But we hear a familiar voice yell, "Ohhhhh, I knew it!"

Rodney runs up to us, followed by agents. Haley slips her tied-together hands over my head. She steps back as Mr. Foster runs up and grabs her in a giant bear hug.

I KNEW IT!

Rodney clasps me in a bear hug too. Wolfshaw breaks through the crowd and clears his throat, commanding our attention.

"Did you catch him?" I ask.

"Saul isn't in the school, but we have agents fanning out around the city. We'll find him."

My heart sinks. Even though I saved the day, I can't help but feel guilty—none of this would have happened if it wasn't for me. Uncle Saul already evaded them for twelve years. He could easily do it again.

"We did recover the capsule, and the list is safe. But, Foster," Wolfshaw says, turning to Haley's dad, "I just got word that there was a break-in at the Black Belt Karate Studio."

"Saul?" he asks.

"We didn't get much on the cameras, but we think it was a woman. Saul may have an accomplice," Wolfshaw says. "He knew that once the capsule was opened, all agents would converge here, including the ones guarding the studio. Looks like it was a classic smash-and-grab—everything from the cabinet in your office was taken."

Mr. Foster looks up, scratching his chin. "I don't

think there was anything too valuable in there. Mostly uniforms and paperwork on our regular karate students, but we'll need to check the inventory list to be sure."

★★★

We call Rodney's mom to let her know that Rodney's spending the night with me and we don't need a ride. Then Rodney, Haley, and I go to the band hall to help clean up the huge mess. Mr. Foster pulls me aside and explains that Rodney will need to be suppressed. Again.

"We'll do it right. Don't worry. He'll just forget about tonight."

I get it. Rodney saw too much, and I trust Gravitas now. Finally.

"What about me? Will I get suppressed too?"

"You'll have to ask Wolfshaw about that."

So I do. I take a deep breath and walk up to the man who told me I wasn't good enough to train, and I ask if I'm getting suppressed.

He shakes his head. "Not at the moment. Perhaps you'll be a valuable Gravitas agent, after all, if you can learn to control yourself. But you put lives in danger by not telling Gravitas about Saul sooner, and you've broken many rules. There are consequences." He hands me a towel and a box of baking soda. "You can start by cleaning up that stain." He points to Uncle Saul's vomit spot, where he yacked earlier, after yanking.

"With great power there must also come—great responsibility."

I have a feeling this won't be my only consequence.

I take the towel and drop to my knees and scrub. Haley and Rodney help the agents restore the band hall so it will look normal by Monday morning. The gravitars pull music stands upright and bits of broken trophies into piles, but all they can do after that is start piecing the trophies back together again, with patience and glue, not superpowers.

Rodney finds his trumpet in the middle of the mess. "Oh man. It got dented again!" he moans.

"Let me see it." Mr. Foster stares at the dent, and the bell begins to straighten. Then he turns the trumpet slowly back and forth, smoothing out the brass until it looks as good as new.

Mr. Foster was right when he told me he had stopped being an agent but hasn't stopped saving the world. Sure, it wasn't the whole world, not this time. But that trumpet is Rodney's world.

Two weeks later, it's finally time for the Starry, Starry Night Christmas Dance. Rodney comes over to my house to get ready, and Mom insists on taking pictures on the front porch before we go.

"Where's Haley?" she asks.

"She's getting picked up by her date."

Andy asked her to go with him, and she said yes. Sure, I would have liked for her to go with Rodney and me like last year, but it's okay. I guess that means I've grown up a little too.

"Technically, her date's mom is taking them," says Rodney.

"Yeah. Haley said there's no way she's walking all the way to school in heels."

"She's wearing heels?" asks Rodney. "If you're The Minor Miracle, that's a major miracle!"

Rodney holds his trumpet in all the pictures. When it's time to go, he's still holding it.

"Do you really have to bring it to the dance? Haley said student council hired a DJ."

"But I have an epic idea." Rodney tells it to me as we walk to the school. "We'll be famous," he promises. "Are you in?"

I grin and give him a fist bump. "I'm in."

"Great! I brought you this." He pulls a floppy rubber chicken out of his jacket and hands it to me.

At the dance, Haley is so busy making sure the whole evening runs according to her schedule that she only dances one and a half dances with Andy—not that I'm counting. And it turns out Andy can't even dance, so they're both fine with that.

Chuck hangs out at the snack table, eating all the cookies, while his date dances with her friends and ignores him. I wonder if he'll barfy, barfy later.

Suddenly, the DJ stops the music. I look to the front of the gym and see Rodney jump onstage, holding his trumpet. It's time.

Everyone slowly stops what they're doing when they realize the music has quit playing. All eyes are on the stage.

Holding the rubber chicken high, I run to join Rodney as he plays the first few notes of the chicken dance song. I drop the rubber chicken and open and close my hands like beaks. Heat rises to my cheeks, but I don't stop. Haley pushes her way toward the stage, and I hope she doesn't shut us down.

Another kid with a trumpet stands up in the bleachers and joins Rodney in playing the next line. I tuck my thumbs under my armpits and waggle my elbows like wings. A few people giggle, and I blush but don't stop. This is for Rodney.

He's playing with his old familiar swagger, and his cheeks are round and full like Dizzy's.

Another trumpet starts to play from the opposite side of the gym, followed by a drum, trombone, clarinets, and flutes. By the end of the first verse, half the band is playing "The Chicken Dance," all spaced out around the gym. I wiggle my hips and clap, willing to look ridiculous for my friend. "First to join me gets the rubber chicken!" I yell.

Some kid starts dancing, and I toss it to him. A few more join, and soon it's like a wave moving back through the student body. The rubber chicken flies through the air as kids toss it around. Haley comes onstage and grabs the microphone from the DJ.

No, Haley, don't mess this up.

"Rim Rock Middle School's first flash mob ever!" she booms, then flaps her elbows with the rest of us.

Soon the whole gym has joined in. I catch Andy squatting and flapping, and even Chuck leaves the cookies and joins his date in a big circle of chicken dancers. Phones are out, their lights like little stars at our Starry, Starry Night dance.

Rodney plays a long, drawn-out note, signaling for the band to wrap up. The whole gym erupts into cheers when they stop playing.

"We did it!" Rodney holds his trumpet up high.

"You're welcome for not shutting it down." Haley's sweaty from dancing, and her ponytail is pulled loose. She still looks perfect.

Rodney grins at her and gives me a fist bump. "You guys can be my sidekicks anytime."

Haley rolls her eyes.

I throw one arm around Rodney, the other around Haley. "You know what? That would be super."

ACKNOWLEDGMENTS

The fact that any manuscript becomes a book on a shelf is a minor miracle, and it can't be done alone.

My writing friends, including Anne, Betty, Lindsey L., Lindsey S., Cyn, Andrea, Dianna, Kathi, Jane, Erin, Debbie, Sam, Julie Ann, Gayleen, Jerri, Paige, and many others, have supported me for years and sent my writing to the next level, leaving their marks on my work and my life. I am so grateful.

Alyssa Eisner Henkin of Birch Path Literary, thank you for swooping in with your wisdom and enthusiasm, your passion for this industry, and your vision for this project and all the others.

At the end of a movie when the credits roll, I'm always astonished by how many people are behind the scenes. As the credits roll on this book, I thank all the teams and individuals: publishing and editorial (Laura Barker, Sarah Rubio, Tina Constable, Campbell Wharton, and Jennifer Reyes), production (Linnea Knollmueller, Jenn Backe, Jessica Heim, and Phil Leung), managing editorial (Chris Tanigawa, Liza Stepanovich, and Julia Wallace), art and design (Sonia Persad and Jenny Davis), copy editor Jessica Lack, proofreading (JoLeigh Buchanan, Kayla Fenstermaker, and Bryan Gordon), production editor Helen Macdonald, marketing (Jess Foggy and Ada Ramos), publicity

(Elizabeth Groening and Levi Phillips), everyone on the sales team, and all the others whose individual names I don't know. You made this book become real, and that's an incredible superpower.

To Billy Yong, when you said yes, I was over the moon . . . the supermoon! Thank you for showing the world what was in my words with your incredible style and creativity.

Bunmi Ishola, thank you for the many careful reads, for breaking this story so it could be stronger, and for giving Noah Minor a chance. Your energy knows no bounds, and your work enables children to fly up, up, and away through the power of story.

And finally, a trillion thanks to my family—my cheering squad that keeps me grounded and humble and grateful and inspired—and especially to my husband, Clay. I would have put his name on the cover if he'd let me. I've gone to him hundreds of times with "what-ifs" and "what abouts." He is a wonder and my most favorite superhero.

ABOUT THE AUTHOR

MEREDITH DAVIS is a wife, mother, and grandmother living in Austin, Texas. She is the founder of the Austin chapter of the Society of Children's Book Writers and Illustrators and holds an MFA in writing for children and young adults from Vermont College of Fine Arts. Her first book, *Her Own Two Feet: A Rwandan Girl's Brave Fight to Walk,* which she co-authored with the super heroic Rebeka Uwitonze, earned a starred review in *Publishers Weekly* and was a Junior Library Guild selection, a nominee for the NAACP Image Award, and *World* magazine's Children's Book of the Year winner for nonfiction. Meredith's superpower is reading, and she defies gravity often, her head in the clouds and her imagination soaring.

ABOUT THE ILLUSTRATOR

BILLY YONG is an illustrator and character designer who loves drawing the sweet and nonsensical. He's been privileged to work on a wide range of projects, from picture books to middle grade novels and even packaging for fish. When he's not doodling around, he's busy surviving parenthood or fighting against his addiction to bubble tea. Billy lives in sunny Singapore.